Christmas 1946.

ρ

G000166252

DRIVEN TO MURDER

DEBBIE YOUNG

Boldwood

First published in Great Britain in 2024 by Boldwood Books Ltd.

Copyright © Debbie Young, 2024

Cover Design by Head Design Ltd

Cover Illustration: Shutterstock

A CIP catalogue record for this book is available from the British Library.

Paperback ISBN 978-1-80483-146-5

Large Print ISBN 978-1-80483-147-2

Hardback ISBN 978-1-80483-148-9

Ebook ISBN 978-1-80483-145-8

Kindle ISBN 978-1-80483-144-1

Audio CD ISBN 978-1-80483-153-3

MP3 CD ISBN 978-1-80483-152-6

Digital audio download ISBN 978-1-80483-150-2

Boldwood Books Ltd
23 Bowerdean Street
London SW6 3TN
www.boldwoodbooks.com

For Laura.

'As if in a dream, he found himself, somehow, seated in the driver's seat; as if in a dream, he pulled the lever and swung the car round the yard and out through the archway; and, as if in a dream, all sense of right and wrong, all fear of obvious consequences, seemed temporarily suspended. He increased his pace, and as the car devoured the street and leapt forth on the high road through the open country, he was only conscious that he was Toad once more, Toad at his best and highest, Toad the terror, the traffic-queller, the Lord of the lone trail, before whom all must give way or be smitten into nothingness and everlasting night.'

— KENNETH GRAHAME – THE WIND IN THE WILLOWS

1

THE BUS STOPS HERE

'So, when would you like to start your driving lessons?'

Hector's playlist of songs on the theme of cars should have put me on my guard. As the opening chords of 'Driving in My Car' by Madness rang out, I put his morning coffee and a shortbread finger on the bookshop's trade counter. It was our first day back from our Scottish holiday, and I was still reacclimatising to being back in Wendlebury Barrow after a week staying with my parents.

'Oh, I don't know. When I get round to it.'

I was already regretting my holiday promise to Hector that I'd learn to drive if he learned to swim. Driving lessons were not my top priority. Far more pressing was preparing to launch the new second-hand department of Hector's bookshop, Hector's House.

Hector dipped the biscuit into his coffee. 'But you've got your provisional licence, haven't you?'

I couldn't deny it. I'd applied for it not long after I'd moved to the village, when I'd inherited my cottage from the late travel writer May Sayers, my great-aunt. Her kind legacy had changed my life, leaving behind my career as a peripatetic teacher of English to non-native speakers in European cities, and enabling me to settle down in this pleasant rural community.

More recently, I'd passed the driving theory test. That was the easy bit.

Next, I had to overcome my aversion to driving. That dated back to when I was living with my ex-boyfriend, Damian. If I'd had a licence, he'd have cajoled me into driving his travelling theatre company's tour bus, so I flatly refused to take driving lessons. That was one area in our few years together on which I'd stood my ground. Besides, the cities in which I worked had excellent public transport – trams, trains and buses – so I didn't need to drive.

Since moving to Wendlebury Barrow, I'd enjoyed being chauffeured everywhere by Hector in his beloved Land Rover. It wasn't much more comfortable than Damian's clapped-out van, but I didn't care.

'Well, yes,' I replied. A promise was a promise, but I could play for time. 'However, before I can go any further, I need to find a decent driving instructor. I'd thought about giving the local guy a ring. I've seen his red hatchback about the village, with the sign on top – "Succeed with Saxon". I expect he's booked up ages in advance though, so no rush.'

Hector turned his doleful lost puppy look on me, green eyes wide beneath his dark curls. 'Why pay good money to a driving instructor when I can teach you? I thought it might be fun to give you your first lesson after work tonight. Look, I've just made you a present.'

From beneath the trade counter, he produced a pair of white cardboard squares, each bearing a large red letter 'L' for 'Learner'. He must have printed them on the shop's laser printer.

that only a couple of years before, when the council was dishing out bus route licences, it had ousted the previous incumbent, dazzled by Highwayman's jazzier livery, upbeat advertising and charismatic young CEO, who made the aging, scruffy head of the old service provider look overdue for retirement.

The passengers decided to take the matter into their own hands, staging imaginative protests, and *The Weekly Slate* had a field day reporting on their antics. When vigilantes daubed 'Daylight Robbery' in big red letters on the side of a Highwayman bus, a photograph filled the front page. A campaigner boarding a bus dressed as eighties pop singer Adam Ant in full highwayman garb gave rise to the headline 'Stand and Deliver'. Thanks to the publicity, that campaigner – by day a milkman – soon had a lucrative sideline as a celebrity lookalike.

When he answered Hector's question regarding the bus being axed, Billy's voice turned mournful. 'They're stopping the whole service at the end of November, just in time to scupper a person's chances of Christmas shopping.'

'Books make wonderful Christmas presents,' I put in. I never miss a sales opportunity – one reason why Hector had offered me a partnership in his shop. I really had made a difference to the bookshop's bottom line in the year I'd worked for him. It's not easy to sustain an independent bookshop in a small Cotswold village, especially outside the tourist season. Needing all the hustles we can get, we were about to add piano lessons to our range of products and services, since Hector had discovered in Scotland that I could play. (Grade 8 with distinction, in case you're wondering.) Hector, who wrote romantic novels on the side, had also encouraged me to pursue my own writing ambitions. I'd got as far as the third volume of my memoirs of village life, *Murder in the Manger*.

'Of course, the cuts won't matter to them that drives,' Billy went on. 'Either cars or those new-fangled electric bikes like Kate Barker's got herself.'

Hector's jaw dropped at the mental image of his affluent, elegant godmother abandoning her sleek convertible sports car for two wheels. 'Kate's got an electric bike?'

'Riding about the place like the Wicked Witch of the West, she is.'

Hector's brow furrowed. 'Surely witches ride broomsticks, not bicycles?'

Billy rolled his eyes at me. 'You know what I'm talking about, don't you, young Sophie?'

I came to his aid. 'You know, Hector. That scene in *The Wizard of Oz* in which Dorothy's grumpy neighbour is swept up by the tornado and carries on cycling in mid-air. At the end, we realise she was also the Wicked Witch of the West.'

Billy scowled. 'I can't even afford an old-fashioned pushbike.'

For that, I was truly grateful. Although Billy still did odd jobs around the village to supplement his state pension, his days of safe cycling were long gone. He'd had to stop tackling ladders a while ago too, and now he engaged local teenage tearaway Tommy Crowe to help with any jobs that involved heights, such as gathering mistletoe from local woodland to sell at Christmas.

'I won't even save money on bus fares, as I don't pay 'em in the first place, thanks to me bus pass.'

An elderly lady who'd been browsing the rack of greeting cards came over to add her tuppence-worth and sat on another chair at Billy's table.

'Scrapping the buses is like a pay-cut for pensioners,' she declared, setting her handbag down on Billy's table. 'Our free bus passes will be worthless now, won't they, Bill? Might as well not bother sending them to us if we can't use 'em.'

As she was about to reply, the shop door creaked open to

admit Maggie Burton, who immediately tuned in to our topic of conversation.

'You telling them about the buses, Hilary?' Maggie didn't wait for her friend's reply. 'I'd been looking forward to getting my first bus pass next birthday, and now they've gone and spoiled it. If we're to do all our grocery shopping at the village shop, we'll all be as thin as Janice Boggins, what with the prices that Carol Barker charges.'

I immediately sprang to the defence of my friend Carol, proprietor of our village shop. 'You can't expect Carol to compete on price with the big supermarkets in Slate Green. They buy stock in such vast quantities that their suppliers give them big discounts, so they can afford to set low prices. Small traders like Carol don't have that advantage.'

Maggie narrowed her eyes. 'That's her story.'

Ever the diplomat, Hector steered the conversation away from slander. 'Thank goodness for the mobile library,' he said. The council's library service bus trundled up the hill from Slate Green once a fortnight and stopped in the car park beside the village hall for an hour. 'At least when you can no longer get the bus to the central library in town, they'll still bring books for you to borrow.'

As Maggie pulled out the last free chair at the table, Billy edged back. Poor Billy, having come in for a quiet coffee and a chat, now found himself in the middle of a budding insurrection.

'There was me looking forward to retirement,' Maggie went on. 'Now it looks as if I'll have to get a job somehow in the village if I'm to go on feeding myself and my cats.'

Billy put a hand over his eyes. 'Don't go bringing your moggies into it. It's not Highwayman's fault if you get pets you can't afford to feed. Besides, you've got your widow's pension.'

Maggie's husband, Frank, had died from a severe case of food poisoning not long before I moved to the village.

'I've one less cat to feed, thanks to Janice Boggins. She's always hated my cats, and now she's out to poison them all. Every time they go next door into her garden, they're sick afterwards, and don't try telling me it's just furballs.'

Hector raised his hands for silence. 'It's not only about money, Billy. Everyone who uses the 27 bus will be sad to see it go, from the kids that use it to get to secondary school to old people who have had to give up driving. The point is, the village needs its bus service.'

I immediately thought of Tommy, the bored and slightly lonely local teenager who often hangs around in Hector's House, despite not being remotely interested in reading. Chatting with Hector and Billy is part of the attraction – Tommy's father left his mother while he was very young, and with only his mother and younger sister, Sina, at home, he seems to crave male company. He's a kind and thoughtful lad who just needs pointing in the right direction, so I do what I can to support him too.

Although Tommy has the best intentions, he's a magnet for trouble, and we've had to fish him out of a few scrapes since I came to the village. Tommy claims never to read books, and has been known to confuse Terry Pratchett with Charles Dickens, judging only by their photographs. We find him odd jobs to make him feel useful, such as breaking up cardboard boxes for recycling, and reward him with free milkshakes from the tearoom. In a few years' time Tommy will leave school and enter the world of work. Who can afford to buy and run a car when they're just starting out? The loss of the bus would severely hamper his employment prospects.

I tried to lift everyone's spirits with my usual optimism.

'I expect the parish council is on the case,' I surmised. 'Maybe they'll be able to persuade the bus company to change its mind.'

Maggie sat up straight, eager to share some news. 'You won't know this, Sophie, as you were away last week, but the parish council has called an emergency public meeting in the village hall for the day after tomorrow. It's so people can state the impact of the cuts to a representative from Highwayman.' She slumped back in her chair again. 'Not that it'll do any good. They still doubled ticket prices last year, despite our petition.'

Billy took a quick slurp of his coffee. 'I reckons the only person who will come out of it better off is ruddy Arch.'

'Who?' I wasn't sure whether that was the name of a person or an organisation – a rival transport company, perhaps.

'You know, Saxon Arch, the driving instructor, big brother of Norman. You must have seen his car driving about the place with that big sign on the top to make people look at him.'

'"Speed with Saxon", that's his motto,' added Maggie. 'Bright red, his car is, to help pedestrians see him coming so they can jump out of his way. Not that Saxon's a bad driver, but you need to watch out when his pupils are behind the wheel.'

I bit back a smile. 'Yes, I've seen him, but I think you'll find his sign says "Succeed", not "Speed with Saxon". I don't think I've ever met him. He's never been in Hector's House, has he, Hector? Not while I've been here, anyway.'

'You don't want him in here, neither,' said Billy. 'Nasty piece of work. Unkind to his poor brother, that good-for-nothing Norman. Not Norman's fault, mind.'

Having moved to the village the summer of the previous year, when I inherited Great-Auntie May's cottage, I'd lived there long enough to know not to fuel local feuds, so I didn't enquire as to Billy's grudge against Saxon Arch. But I was curious as to whether he'd be a viable driving instructor.

'I'm learning to drive.' I hoped that remark would trigger some feedback on Saxon Arch's merits as a teacher, without my having to ask outright at risk of offending Hector.

'Then you don't want to get in a car with that Saxon,' retorted Billy. 'My second cousin's niece did, and as a result, she ended up in the family way.'

Hilary leaped to Saxon's defence. 'Yes, but only after she married him. They just fell for each other during her driving lessons. Really, Bill, you're the worst gossipmonger I've ever known.'

She got up from her seat and picked up her handbag and the greetings card she'd chosen. She turned to Hector. 'I'd like to pay for this card now, if I may, Hector.'

'Certainly.'

Hector returned to his post, and I took that as a cue to retreat to the tearoom counter.

I was cross with Billy for upsetting Hilary; I'd been about to offer her the tearoom menu.

'Any drinks or cakes for you, Maggie?' I called hopefully, as she and Billy leaned towards each other, deep in conversation in voices too low for me to understand.

Maggie glanced at me and shook her head, whispered a few more words to Billy, then left the shop without so much as looking at a book.

* * *

After our last customer of the day had left, Hector locked the front door.

'We'll get more of that once the bus service stops,' declared Hector, flipping the door sign to 'closed'.

'More of what?' I switched off the coffee machine at the mains.

'People like Maggie Burton using the shop as a free social gathering place, with no intention of spending any money.'

I put the tub of butter pats in the fridge. 'That's okay, though, isn't it? It's not as if it costs anything for people to browse. They're bound to buy something eventually.'

Hector disappeared beneath the trade counter for a moment as he bent to power down the computer and printer.

'I suppose so.' He stood up, straightened his back and stretched his arms above his head, his stomach taut beneath his soft grey lambswool sweater.

'Try to look on the bright side,' I urged him. 'In the long term, once the bus stops running, we'll probably sell a lot more books to villagers unable to go to town to buy birthday and Christmas presents. Plus, they'll meet their friends for coffee in our tearoom instead of going into Slate Green. Having more people in the shop will make it look busier, and a busy shop will attract more paying customers. No one ever likes to go into an empty shop, but a full shop draws in passers-by with FOMO. And then we pounce!' I bared my teeth and raised my hands, curling my fingers in an impression of a tiger's claws. 'Then you sell them a ton of books and I stuff them full of tea and cakes!'

Hector smiled but shook his head. 'You're forgetting about the internet. People will still be able to shop online, bus or no bus.'

I flicked off the light switch that served the tearoom. 'Well, here's another grain of comfort. Doesn't each human body generate a certain amount of heat?'

'About a hundred watts when at rest, I believe.'

'Well, then, in the depths of winter, with a shop full of customers, we'll save money on our heating bill.'

With a sigh, Hector reached for our coats from the rack behind the counter. When I came over to join him, he held mine out to help me on with it.

'Okay, enough of the optimism, Pollyanna.'

I frowned. 'Sorry. And to be honest, I feel churlish for planning how the shop might benefit from the village losing its bus service. I'd still rather the bus service kept going.'

'It's not just shoppers who will suffer,' said Hector. 'People need it to get to medical appointments and to work, and the older kids need it to get to the high school in Slate Green. I used to do that myself, and the bus journey was an important part of the whole cultural experience of going to big school.'

Hector had been born and raised in Wendlebury, where his parents ran an antique shop, only leaving to go to university. Then he'd worked as a bookseller in various towns to support his girlfriend Celeste, who had become seriously ill when they were travelling abroad together. When she had recovered and left him, he'd moved back to Wendlebury Barrow. His parents were about to retire from running their antique shop, and he'd taken it over and transformed it into a bookshop. This project provided the stability he needed in the comfort of his home turf. There he had settled ever since, and now was as well-versed in the ways of the Wendlebury Barrow community as if he'd never been away.

'Plus, anyone out of work, like Norman Arch, needs the bus to get to the jobcentre,' he continued. 'If they don't sign on every fortnight, they lose their unemployment benefit. I'm sure in a community like this, kind neighbours with cars will rally round and offer lifts when they can, but it's not pleasant for people to lose their independence at any age. So, the sooner you gain your driving licence the better, then you can be part of that pool of volunteer drivers. How about we start with your first lesson right now?'

My heart sank as Hector set the burglar alarm. All day I'd been toying with suggesting a trade-off about the mutual pledge we'd made in Scotland. I'd let Hector off his promise to learn to swim, provided he didn't pressure me to learn to drive. I'd got used to him driving me everywhere, and I rather liked it. Plus, I wasn't sure how easy I'd find it. I didn't want to embarrass myself in front of Hector by taking ages to learn or by failing the test. Now it seemed there was no way out. I just hoped having Hector as my driving instructor wouldn't wreck our relationship.

2

SOPHIE GOES OFF-ROAD

As Hector climbed into the driver's seat, I was feeling slightly less daunted. At least he wasn't expecting me to drive his precious Land Rover out of its parking space beside the book-shop and onto the High Street. A condemned prisoner may be grateful for even the shortest stay of execution.

As Hector buckled his seat belt, his expression was morose. 'I don't know. We leave the village for a week, and everything falls apart.'

'It's hardly everything,' I protested, fastening mine. 'Besides, there have been some positive changes too, like Ted and Carol getting engaged. I'm so happy for them.'

Unlike me, Carol was more than ready for marriage.

'It's only really the bus service that's changing,' I continued. 'Oh, and Kate getting an electric bike is a new development, but that's hardly a threat to our business. Good for her, I say, and good for the environment. That fancy car of hers must be a real gas-guzzler.' I hoped learning to drive wasn't going to turn me into a boring petrol head. 'Otherwise, everything else seems pretty much as we left it.'

Hector remained silent, lips pursed, so I prattled on, hoping to lift his spirits. 'I like cycling. That cycle ride we had last week along the towpath of the Caledonian Canal was lovely.'

Hector turned the key in the ignition and did something with the gearstick. 'Until that mad old woman nearly drove me off the cycle path and into the canal.'

He wrenched the handbrake far harder than usual. I bit my lip.

'Sorry, Hector, your little accident slipped my mind for a moment. Still, it was a lovely cycle ride up till then, wasn't it? So, I was thinking, maybe instead of learning to drive, I could get an electric bike like Kate's. I wonder whether you can get them with big wicker baskets on the front, like old-fashioned butchers' boys' delivery bikes? We could attach an enamel sign with the shop's name and details. Everywhere I cycled, I'd be advertising Hector's House for free.'

We turned onto the high street and then headed north down a lane that soon narrowed to a single track with the occasional passing place. I wound my window down, breathing in the damp evening air. It smacked of decay. The tangle of brambles in the hedgerows, their leaves tinged with a rusty brown, had long been stripped of blackberries by locals planning to make jam and by wildlife fattening themselves up against the barren winter.

'Where are we going? I presume you're taking me some-where without much traffic for my first driving lesson, but I'd prefer a bit more space on either side of the car.'

The hedgerows were so close to the Land Rover on both sides that if I hadn't been wary of their savage thorns, I could have reached out and touched them.

I checked Hector's expression in the rear-view mirror. He was looking awfully serious.

'Don't worry, so would I,' he replied. 'Land Rovers may be built like tanks, but that doesn't mean you can steamroller over everything in your tracks. I'm taking you to the old airfield at Eyebright, where absolutely nothing can get in your way.'

I blinked in surprise. 'What about the aeroplanes?'

'Especially not the aeroplanes. Since the gliding club closed, all the aeroplanes have gone elsewhere. It was only the club members' storage fees and landing licences that kept the airfield viable for private pilots. Now it's just an empty wasteland.'

As a yellow hatchback approached, Hector steered expertly into a passing place. When he raised his palm to acknowledge its driver's thanks for giving way, I did the same, practising for when it was my turn to drive.

Hector's lips twitched in amusement as the hatchback passed us, and he pulled back onto the lane. 'That's a hand signal you won't find in the Highway Code,' he observed. 'But it's an essential courtesy driving round these lanes. It's always a good idea to be polite on these single-track roads.'

'Why, does being polite make you drive better?'

In the rear-view mirror, I saw his eyes crease with mirth. 'No, because you might encounter someone you know. Modern polarised windscreens make it hard to tell who the driver is until you get close to an oncoming car, especially in a vehicle like this, where the driver sits relatively high. So, remember, Sophie, never make rude or impatient gestures at an approaching car, no matter how badly you think they're driving. You might find out when you get closer that it's the vicar at the wheel.'

I'd hate to offend our gentle vicar, the Reverend Gerard Murray.

Hector slowed at a crossroads with another single-track lane before turning left. An old-fashioned cast-iron fingerpost told us we were two miles from Eyebright. In an attempt to allay my nerves, I kept talking.

'So, going back to what you were saying about everything falling apart, what else have you discovered? There's nothing wrong at your flat, is there?'

I was hoping he hadn't found a burst pipe or other domestic disaster that might delay our plans for setting up the second-hand department. Since our return from Scotland, I'd only been in his flat briefly to try the piano he'd had shipped from his parents' home while we were away. I'd been eager to spend the first night back in my cottage with Blossom, a sweet little black kitten, almost full-grown now, that Billy had given me the previous Easter. Over his morning coffee, like a magician he'd produced her from the pocket of his ancient tweed jacket. She was a well-intentioned gift I couldn't refuse.

I'd also wanted to thank my elderly next-door neighbour, Joshua, for feeding her while I was away. Tommy would have fed Blossom if I'd asked. He's always keen to earn pocket money. But I thought giving Joshua a reason to leave his cottage every day would be good for him. Fond of Blossom, Joshua was always pleased when she visited his garden, a generous attitude for a keen gardener, considering her main reason for going there.

'Don't worry, my flat is just as I left it,' said Hector. 'I'm just saddened by the news about the bus service. I keep thinking of how its loss will affect so many people. I'm lucky, I have my own wheels, and you'll be driving soon, too. But for so many people, that's not an option.'

Hector had been so upbeat on our journey back down south; I was sorry to see him downhearted now.

'It is a shame, but as I was saying earlier, maybe it'll make more people spend more money at our shop and tearoom instead.'

I tingled with pride as I realised this was the first time I'd referred to Hector's House as 'our' shop rather than his. Although we had yet to formalise our business partnership, I was already feeling proprietorial.

Hector slowed down for a hairpin bend. 'The thing is, most library users also buy books, but few can afford to buy as many books as they borrow from a library. It may bring us a little more trade, but I'm still sad for library users. They'll miss the social side of the library as well as the books, and the banter with the librarians. The library staff are like real friends to borrowers. No, they *were* real friends to the community they serve. They knew all their borrowers by name. There are almost certain to be job losses too for those who have no alternative transport to get to work. It's not as if they'll find alternative employment in the village.'

Local jobs were scarce, and I was grateful I'd been lucky enough to get my job at Hector's House not long after I'd moved to Wendlebury. I didn't even get it on my own merits, as I found out only some time later that Hector had taken me on as a belated thank-you to Auntie May, who had helped him financially when he'd set up the shop a few years before. This knowledge made me determine to prove myself a valuable employee. I was pleased and proud that my efforts had paid off.

Although Auntie May had left me her cottage, delivering me from the need to pay rent and transforming me overnight into a homeowner when a mortgage would have been beyond my reach, I needed a job to afford to run it. If it hadn't been for Hector's kind offer, I'd have been one of the locals commuting to Slate Green and left in the lurch by the cancellation of the bus service.

We were approaching a weathered wooden sign, nailed to the split trunk of huge dead oak tree. I guessed the tree had met its demise at the end of a lightning fork. No wonder the gliding club had abandoned the site. If I'd seen that reminder of the fatal powers of the elements every time I came here to fly a plane, I would have thought twice before taking off.

Hector steered onto the rutted, muddy track. At the far end, amid lush green pasture, stood a disused aircraft hangar the colour of a Rich Tea biscuit. I wished he'd brought me here in the spring when pollinators buzzing over a carpet of wildflowers would have seemed like the ghosts of past aircraft.

Beyond the hangar, the flat track straightened out into a long strip for take-off and landing. Apart from occasional tufts of ripe wheat, presumably inadvertently planted by birds passing overhead, it looked in better repair than some of the multi-potholed lanes that criss-crossed our part of the Cotswolds.

'Wow, it's so straight it could be an old Roman road, like the Fosse Way. If it wasn't for the old aircraft hangar. And the control tower. And the warning signs for low-flying aircraft.'

Hector laughed as he slowed the Land Rover to a halt and applied the handbrake. After shoving the gear stick forward, he switched off the ignition, unfastened his seat belt, opened the door and jumped down onto the tarmac.

'Come on then, now's your big moment. All change.'

I unclipped my seat belt and took a deep breath. Then I swung my legs over the gear stick and wriggled across to plant my bottom in the driving seat. When Hector climbed into the passenger seat, it felt odd to see him on that side of the vehicle.

Once we'd fastened our seat belts, Hector shuffled round to face me. I gripped the steering wheel, my hands at the 'ten to two' clockface position, which I'd read somewhere was what driving examiners looked for. Or was it 'twenty to four'?

When I compromised with a quarter to three, Hector

covered my hands with his and moved them five minutes north on either side. I stared straight ahead.

Now that I had this nice, easy, empty road ahead of me, I was eager to begin, but unsure what to do next. To disperse surplus nervous energy, I bounced up and down in my seat a couple of times. Then I took my eyes off the road to look at Hector, hoping for some clues.

'So, shall I start her up? How do I do that? Do I just turn the key?'

Hector snorted. 'Hold your horses, sweetheart. You're not going anywhere until you know which pedal is which.'

Talk about patronising! I tightened my grip on the steering wheel to control the urge to punch him. Oblivious to my injured pride, he pointed at the floor.

'Just remember, the pedals are in alphabetical order by function. A, B, C: accelerator, brake, clutch.'

'Copy that!' I replied brightly, the airfield setting going to my head. Now I imagined taking flight, like Chitty Chitty Bang Bang. Once I'd mastered driving, perhaps I could learn to fly a plane.

I tapped each pedal, from left to right, with the tip of my right shoe. 'Accelerator, brake, clutch.'

Hector facepalmed. 'No, no, Sophie, other way round. Like I said, A, B, C.'

When he pointed at the pedals again, I realised he was going from right to left. I thumped the steering wheel.

'Oh, for goodness' sake, make your mind up! That's *reverse* alphabetical order. In this country, we read from left to right. It's C, B, A.'

'That's why I pointed, so you could see which pedal was which.' He wagged his finger in the air. 'You know what I mean. Same difference.'

I scowled. 'It's not the same thing at all. You'd soon complain if I sorted our fiction section in reverse alphabetical order.'

Hector closed his eyes, took a deep breath and exhaled slowly. 'Okay, moving swiftly on. We've established that from left to right we have clutch, brake and accelerator. I take it you know what each one does.'

I huffed. 'Of course I do. I'm not stupid. I've been a passenger enough times. The accelerator makes you go faster, and the brake makes you slow down. Just like on the dodgems at the Village Show. Easy-peasy.'

'And the clutch?'

I hesitated, staring at the mystery pedal. 'It – it clutches things. It – oh, I don't know.'

I slapped the steering wheel again, this time in frustration. 'How did having cars with three pedals ever catch on when drivers only ever have two legs at most? Your piano has only two pedals. Although grand pianos have three, but I've barely played one of those. And how anyone ever copes with the gazillion pedals on a church organ is beyond me.'

Hector refused to be diverted. 'The clutch allows you to disengage the gearbox from the engine so you can change gear. Once you've changed gear, you release the clutch to reengage the engine and continue driving.'

I couldn't argue with that, because I didn't really understand it, but I wasn't going to confess that to Hector.

When it felt as if he'd been banging on about gears for about half an hour, he finally gave me permission to start the engine. It took me only moments to run the Land Rover off the tarmac and come to a juddering halt in long grass.

I forced an apologetic smile. 'It's a good thing it's an all-terrain vehicle,' I said, high-pitched.

Hector took another deep breath in and out. 'Let's try that again.'

I pointed across the field. 'Oh look, there's a rabbit! Look, a little brown one! And another.'

'Concentrate, Sophie! Please listen carefully to what I'm saying. Don't let the wildlife distract you, or you'll be more likely to hit them.'

I folded my arms. 'Then perhaps we'd better go elsewhere. I'd hate to run over a rabbit.'

'Listen, we're not driving on a public highway until you've mastered the basics here, where there's no traffic. We're very lucky to have access to such a clear straight road to get you off to a good start. But if you're too tired this evening, we'll pack it in now and go home. We're both weary after our long journey home yesterday, and after going straight back to work today with no rest day in between.'

Without waiting for my permission, he unlatched his seat belt, opened the door and jumped out onto the grass.

As I wriggled back over into the passenger seat, a sense of failure lodged like a stone in the pit of my stomach. Trying to distract myself, I gazed at the bunnies dashing about the field. They can't have liked having a noisy vehicle on their territory. They must have been several generations on from any wild rabbits who had lived there when it was a working airfield. They would have had no memory of planes taking off and landing, used only to the gentle natural sounds of the countryside.

Hector steered the Land Rover back onto the runway, then executed an annoyingly perfect three-point turn to take us back to the entrance. In silence we drove back through the winding lanes and on to Wendlebury Barrow, where he reversed neatly into his usual parking space. Sensing he was less than pleased with my performance, I tried to regain his favour by talking shop.

'I think it's really good timing to be opening our new second-hand department now,' I said, as we climbed the stairs to his flat. 'It'll enable us to offer more affordable books than those in the main shop to anyone missing the Slate Green library.'

'I suppose so,' said Hector, heading for his kitchenette to fetch a bottle of wine from the fridge. 'But to make the new department work, we'll need to make a lot of trips away from the shop to acquire stock. So, the sooner you learn to drive, Sophie, the better the business will do.'

I gulped. With only a month to go until our planned opening date, I was going to have to try harder if I was to pull my weight as his business partner. Perhaps I'd need to call in reinforcements. I could still allow Hector to teach me to drive, but a little extra instruction from Saxon Arch in between times would enable me to learn more quickly. While Hector stepped out to use the bathroom, I googled Saxon Arch's website. I'd got as far as browsing his online calendar to pick a slot for my first lesson, when I heard the toilet flush. Straight away, I shoved my phone in my back pocket. After all, Hector need never know.

3

TWO PLUS ONE EQUALS FIVE

'Before we can go any further with the new department, we need to recruit some extra part-time staff,' declared Hector as we were opening for business the next morning.

My heart sank. Last time he'd engaged someone to work alongside us in the shop, he'd recruited a beautiful gap year student, Anastasia, without consulting me. That had sent me into paroxysms of jealousy. I hoped Anastasia wasn't on his list of potential employees. On the plus side, at least he was now involving me in the decision.

'Anyone particular in mind?'

'Ted seems to have done well enough covering for us during our trip to Scotland.' That was a relief. No competition there. 'He's popular in the village, so he's one option, provided Carol can spare him.'

Carol, in her fifties, had given up hope of finding romance until Ted, a freelance baker, had pitched up at the village shop the previous autumn with sample cakes for her to try. His cakes were awful, but he turned out to be a brilliant bread maker, so she took him on as a supplier without realising he'd developed a secret crush on her. Ted was too shy to ask her out himself, so I'd fixed them up on a blind date on Valentine's Day, and they'd been going out together ever since. Finding romance in a village, especially later in life, is not easy, and they were lucky to have found each other, with a little help from their friendly local Cupid here.

I wondered whether Ted's temporary job at Hector's House while we were in Scotland, while Mrs Wetherley covered the tea room, was indirectly responsible for their engagement. Perhaps it had caused Carol to fear Ted was slipping away from her. Had that prompted her to propose? The impetus had certainly come from her: she'd told me she'd even gone down on one knee in the pub, after booking the same table they'd had on their blind date. I was very pleased for them, and particularly for Carol, finally putting her own needs first after devoting the earlier part of her adulthood to caring for her aging and infirm parents.

Hector flicked on the power switches of his computer and printer. The familiar low drone of their internal fans, plus the whirr of my coffee machine and the gentle bubbling of my water heater, provided the soundtrack to the start of our working day, until Hector masked them with music. He liked to choose pieces to suit the interests of our customers, deftly navigating his Spotify menu for something appropriate as each new shopper arrived.

Now he settled down on his stool, watching his monitor as the machine went through its start-up process.

'I'll create a job ad once this thing's up and running, and we'll see who turns up. I doubt we'll have problems filling the vacancy. Anyone currently dependent on the bus service to work part-time in Slate Green should be glad of a job on their doorstep.'

As I began setting the tearoom tables with fresh condiments, serviettes and cutlery, I noticed Hector's godmother, Kate, gliding past the shop window on her new electric bike, serene as a swan on a lake in midsummer. She didn't even need to pedal, making the most of the bike's battery. Billy had got it all wrong about the Wicked Witch of the West. She didn't look the slightest bit scary.

Hector must have seen her too, because he leaned back on his wooden stool and clicked a few buttons on his keyboard, making the young Judy Garland's voice begin to ring out around the shop. Then he got up and headed for the stockroom.

A moment later, Maggie Burton breezed into the shop, clearly on a mission. I frowned at the stockroom door, which had just closed behind Hector. Had Hector seen her coming?

'Morning, Sophie, I'm after a birthday present for my nine-year-old god-daughter,' she said, peering over the top of the trade counter as if to make sure Hector wasn't tucked away out of sight somewhere. I noticed the sounds of Hector unboxing the new stock had ceased the minute Maggie's voice sang out.

Maggie's requests were always challengingly vague, but she was a good and loyal customer, and we always did our best to solve her enigmatic book searches. I decided Hector shouldn't get out of dealing with her so easily.

'Hector's just in the stockroom,' I said loudly, intending Hector to hear.

'No need to bother Hector,' she trilled. 'I know exactly what I want.'

That would have been a first. I bit my lip to suppress a smirk.

Then Hector did the decent thing and emerged from the stockroom, a new book in his hand, as if to prove he'd been doing something useful rather than just avoiding Maggie Burton.

'Morning, Maggie.' He forced a smile. 'You're wanting the

children's section. I think you know where it is? Don't worry if the book you're after isn't on the shelves. I can order it in for you from our distributor and have it here in a day or two.'

'Thank you, Hector. No need to trouble yourself. I'll find it in no time.'

She circled the shop floor several times before stopping in front of the children's section. Meanwhile, the school-run mums had been trickling in, heading for their favourite tearoom tables.

'The author's name is to do with Christmas.'

Maggie wasn't addressing Hector or me or anyone in particular, but she spoke loud enough to be heard above the mums' chatter. (I say mums, but there is usually a dad or two and often a few grandparents in the throng.)

'Holly Webb,' suggested one of the mums. 'Writes lots of animal books for kids.'

'How about Ivy Compton-Burnett?' said another. 'Though she's a bit grown-up for even the brightest nine-year-old. She's quite fallen out of vogue these days, which is a shame.'

Maggie shook her head. 'Her first name's definitely Holly, not Ivy. And her surname makes me think of atlases.'

'World,' said a grandma.

'Mercator,' said another. Her kids must have found her a whizz at helping with their geography homework.

'Where's it set?' asked a dad in running gear.

'London,' said Maggie. 'That I'm sure about.'

'Holly A to Z,' he replied deadpan, triggering a ripple of giggles around the tearoom. 'Holly Roadmap.'

Maggie considered. 'Hmm, that doesn't sound quite right.'

'So, what is the book about?' asked the grandma.

Maggie tapped her lips with the fingers of one hand. 'A family of dancers. Well, one of them is a dancer. And none of them are related.'

The tearoom customers looked at each other in tacit amusement. Then Hector cracked and strolled calmly over to join Maggie by the children's section. Crouching down, he pulled a book with a sugar-pink cover off the lowest shelf and held it up to show Maggie, then the tearoom, eliciting a chorus of 'Aah!'

Maggie Burton beamed. 'Ah yes, just what I said! *Ballet Shoes* by Noel Streatfeild. Thank you!'

As Hector returned to the till, Maggie Burton trotted behind him like an adoring puppy. While he was scanning the barcode, she leaned over the counter without a care for his personal space. He quickly reached across the desk to flip over whatever it was she was trying to read. I assumed it was the printed manuscript of his current work-in-progress, *The Kiss of the Sun*. Only after she'd gone, and I was setting a cup of tea on his desk for him, did I check what he'd been so keen to hide. It was the shorthand pad on which he'd been outlining the details of the job advertisement for the ten-till-two vacancy. I just hoped it wasn't going to inspire her to apply for the job herself. Although arguably, Maggie Burton would have been a more suitable applicant than the one who turned up the next day.

4

A NORMAN INVASION

Just after midday, the shop door was flung open so hard that it didn't even creak before it crashed against the wall. The accompanying rush of air rustled the posters on the noticeboard behind the door.

'I hear there's a vacancy,' declared a stocky man in his twenties with florid cheeks. His sandy hair clung to his head in crinkles as tight as a flapper's Marcel wave. 'I'd like to apply.'

Hector, seeming to recognise him, leaped up from his stool and stood straight-backed, stiff-legged. He reminded me of Blossom defending her territory.

'Norman Arch,' he said evenly. 'Yes, we've a vacancy, but not in your line of work.'

Undeterred, Norman Arch came further into the shop, slamming the door behind him. He pressed thick-fingered, square-palmed hands flat on the counter, making the muscles in his forearms bulge. As he leaned forward, Hector took a step back.

'Listen, Hector Munro, I didn't think you'd need a bus driver. Driving buses isn't all I can do. I heard Maggie Burton telling Carol Barker just now that you're looking for a part-time shop assistant. I could do that. I used to handle cards and cash all the time selling tickets to my passengers. Bus drivers don't just drive buses, you know.'

'Yes, but do you have any experience selling books?' Hector said evenly.

Hector must have known he didn't, but it was more diplomatic to make Norman see for himself the job wouldn't be right for him, rather than just rejecting him out of hand.

Norman ignored his question. 'Maggie said the job might include accommodation, as you'll be moving in with Sophie once you open your new second-hand department in your flat.'

Hector did a double take. 'Maggie Burton said that?'

This was news to me too. I almost dropped the stack of plates I was clearing from a tearoom table. I set them down on the counter and went over to join the conversation.

'Hector, did you really say that to Maggie Burton?' I hadn't meant for my voice to come out as a squeak.

Hector chewed his lower lip for a moment. 'No, sweetheart, I've no idea where Maggie got that notion from. Norman, I'm afraid she's sent you here under a misapprehension.'

'On which count?' I asked him, hoping he would assume my question was for Norman Arch's benefit.

I tried to sound carefree. It was one thing to invite Hector to stay the night at my cottage now and again – and we spend about as much time in his flat as in my cottage – but it was another matter to have him move in.

I bit a thumbnail. Was I being hypocritical for accepting an equal partnership in his business without offering him a similar stake in my home? Not that this is common business practice: personal life and work are usually far more separate than ours.

'On both counts, as far as Norman's enquiry is concerned,' Hector replied.

That last clause made me realise that he hadn't ruled out the idea of moving in with me, even if it wasn't at the top of his to-do list. But were either of us ready for that level of commitment?

Hector turned back to Norman. 'I'm sorry, but there's no question of subletting my flat. Besides, most of it will be taken up with shop floor space now.'

Norman began to tap his left foot with the rat-a-tat-tat rhythm of a machine gun. 'I only want one room. Unlike some people's, my needs are modest. It's all right for you, you've got your own business and a flat and a car. Well, if you can call a Land Rover a car.'

Hector bridled at that last remark.

'I just need a room, and as soon as possible,' Norman continued. 'My landlady in Slate Green's about to turf me out. My brother said I can sleep on his sofa, but I won't give him the satisfaction of being able to sneer at me each night as he goes off to tuck himself into his king-size. Otherwise, my only option is to move back into my old childhood bedroom at Mum's. I shouldn't have to be moving back into my mum's house at my age. She's not exactly tickled about it either. If Saxon really wanted to help me, he'd have let me go in with him on his driving instructor business when he set it up.'

When he folded his arms tightly across his chest, I could picture him as a little boy competing with his big brother.

'Mean git. One minute he's moaning about having more bookings than he can fit in his diary, next minute he's saying he hasn't got enough to justify hiring me as a second driver for his business. So, here I am, my job with Highwayman down the toilet, turfed out of my flat, having to apply for any work I can get within walking distance of my mum's.'

'I thought Highwayman's bus service wasn't ending until the start of December?' I queried.

Too late, Hector shot me a warning glance.

Norman clapped his hands together so loudly that I let out a little shriek of alarm. The anger bottled up inside him began to express itself through a repertoire of physical tics. A twitch started up at the outer corner of his right eye, and he kept licking his lips, the tip of his tongue flickering in and out like a snake's.

When Norman turned his attention on me, I slipped behind the trade counter to stand beside Hector, glad of the wooden barrier between us and this strange, unhappy man. For the first time, I wished we had an acrylic shield above the counter, like they do in banks and ticket offices.

A clatter outside the door delayed his reply. Kate was parking her electric bike against the shop front. Then she breezed into the shop, all smiles, to stand beside Norman Arch, patiently waiting her turn in the queue.

Norman did not return her smile of greeting but continued his tirade.

'Oh no, my job with Highwayman went belly up months ago, when that scrawny old cow Janice Boggins dobbed me up. Honestly, I could throttle the old bat for getting me sacked.'

Sensing our discomfort, Kate chipped in with a soothing tone. 'Such a shame for poor Norman to lose his job. The tribunal was a fiasco. But Norman, please remember the vicar and I have both said we'll give you a character reference for any future job applications.'

Norman turned to glare at Kate. 'A fat lot of good a character reference will do if there are no jobs to apply for. No joy with this one.' He jerked his thumb in Hector's direction. 'Driving buses is all I'm good for, so he thinks.'

'And a very good bus driver you were too,' purred Kate. 'Have you thought of casting your net wider? Why not try the bus service operation in Bristol or Cirencester or even Cheltenham? They have far more buses than we do around here. I've seen plenty of buses with recruitment drivers on their rear hoarding whenever I've been in any of those towns. The company that used to run our local bus service is based in Dorset. Doesn't your sister live down that way? I hear they're currently expanding.'

Norman scowled. 'If I want to do that, I need a place to live down there. Without a car I can't commute, and there's no way I can afford to run a car on my dole money. And once the 27 bus disappears, I won't even have my dole, as I won't be able to get to Slate Green to sign on, unless I walk. Why should a grown man in this day and age have to walk eight miles there and back just to get what's his legal right? It ain't fair. I won't do it.'

Kate laid a reassuring hand on his elbow, which is more than I'd have dared do. He shook it off, shuddering.

'Surely your brother will give you a lift. It's only once a fort-night, and I can't believe he has pupils every hour of the day.'

Kate's soothing tone didn't lighten his mood.

'My brother wouldn't give me a lift if his life depended on it,' he snapped. 'Honestly, I don't know what this village is coming to.'

With that, he elbowed Kate out of his way and stomped out of the shop, slamming the door behind him.

For a moment, we basked in the silence. Then my curiosity got the better of me.

'So there really are two brothers in the village named Norman and Saxon Arch?'

Kate nodded, a twinkle in her eye. 'Yes, and they're equally stroppy so-and-sos. Just wait until you meet their sisters, Gothic and Perpendicular.'

Hector tutted at what must have been a tired old joke in

village circles, but it was the first time I'd heard it, and it made me laugh.

'And I suppose the Column family are their cousins?' I added. 'Doric and Ionic, and little baby Corinthian.'

'You might call them pillars of the community.' When Kate shrieked with laughter, even Hector raised a smile. 'Actually, although it's lovely to see you both,' she continued, 'I've popped in to meet a friend for coffee and cake.' She glanced about the tearoom. 'But I'm a little early.'

Hector sat down on his stool, his elbows on the counter, and leaned towards her. 'Good, then you'll just have time to give us the low-down on Norman Arch's disgrace. If you were involved in his tribunal, you must know all the gory details.'

'Hector, you old gossip!' I admonished him, but moved closer to hear whatever Kate was about to tell him.

'You mean with the bus company?' Kate wrinkled her nose in disdain. 'Oh, it was an awful business, and not really his fault at all. Mrs Boggins kept making complaints to the depot manager, accusing Norman of inappropriate behaviour. All he was guilty of was trying to reinforce the company rules about no food and drink on the buses. I don't know whether you've ever been on a bus with Mrs Boggins, but she never travels without some kind of picnic. That day, she was working her way through a bag of hard-boiled eggs, and you know how they reek in an enclosed space.

'Besides, when you eat or drink anything on a bus trundling along our winding lanes, there are bound to be spillages and scraps scattered on the floor. That's why they ban food and drink on board. But when Norman's manager tackled him about Mrs Boggins' complaints, Norman flew into a rage and ended up thumping him. That was completely out of order, and a great shame, because until then he'd had the moral high ground.

There was no way the bus company was going to let him keep his job after that, accusing him of gross misconduct. But now we know they'd planned to axe his route all along, I wonder whether they just wangled his sacking to avoid having to pay him redundancy when the time came.'

The sound of a car pulling up and parking outside the shop distracted Kate's attention. She crossed to the door to wave to the driver of the bright yellow VW Beetle.

'Ah, here's my friend now. We'll have to finish this conversation later.'

She opened the door to admit an elegant middle-aged lady in a pewter trouser suit, a silver woollen stole draped about her shoulders against the autumn chill. I returned to the tearoom to serve them, feeling more grateful than ever that I had a job I loved in the village, within walking distance of my cottage. Then, as I spooned Earl Grey tea leaves into the pot, it dawned on me that all I needed to complete my happiness was that the man I loved should share my cosy cottage too. But how would Hector feel about that? And how could I raise the issue without risking a rejection that might jeopardise our relationship at work? On a practical level, how would he fit his stuff in it, when it was already full of May's souvenirs of her travels around the world? I hadn't expected our new business partnership to cause more problems than it solved.

5

ACTION STATIONS

After I'd served Kate and her friend, as there was no one else in the tearoom, I decided to pop to the village shop for a few essentials that had run low while we'd been away.

I'd already called in on my way to work to congratulate Carol on her engagement, so I anticipated a quick, purposeful visit now, without getting drawn into one of Carol's convoluted conversations. Alas, I was wrong. Carol had a week's worth of pent-up village news to share with me, quite apart from her new status with Ted.

As she chattered away, I was almost overcome by a sickly-sweet smell emanating from two large wicker baskets on the floor beside the counter, overflowing with apples on the cusp of rotting. Carol saw me looking askance at them.

'All donated by Maggie Burton,' she explained. 'They're the last of the season. She said I could keep the proceeds of any sales for the shop, so I could hardly refuse them.'

Then she went back to describing her concerns about the bus service. Like me, Carol didn't drive, but Ted ran a small van for his bread deliveries, so at least she had access to that. But still she wanted to regale me with fond anecdotes of past bus journeys. They dated back to when she was a schoolgirl, struggling to carry home a violin, a cookery basket and her satchel. Later, as a grown-up Christmas shopping in town for her parents, she begrudged being charged an extra fare for the huge turkey she'd wedged into the seat beside her.

'Of course, the bus drivers from those days have long since retired,' she said. 'It's the younger generation losing their jobs I feel sorry for. It was bad enough when that poor Arch boy lost his job. Now the new fellow who replaced him will be for the chop too. Not that he's from Wendlebury.'

As if that made his sacking any less of a shame.

'Kate's just been telling me about Norman Arch's dismissal,' I told her. 'She seemed to think there was some kind of miscarriage of justice.'

Eyeing the queue of customers forming behind me, Carol rang up my milk, sugar and sweetener on the till.

'It was all Janice Boggins' fault,' the lady queuing behind me grumbled. 'Poor Norman was only doing his job. But that wretched company always puts its customers first.'

That was an interesting disconnect. Surely that could only be a good thing?

'There's an idea, Carol,' said a deep, ironic voice behind her. 'Get a wriggle on, love. I only want a packet of ciggies.'

I turned to give an apologetic smile, feeling partly responsible for holding him up. Then, when I saw the source of the voice, I took a step back. It was the near-double of Norman Arch, only with a darker shade of the same crinkly hair and reeking so strongly of cigarette smoke that for a moment I could no longer smell the rotting apples.

The lady standing between us seemed to know him. 'Don't you agree, Saxon? Your brother was robbed of that job.'

Saxon shrugged. 'He should have taken our dad's advice, like I did, and set up on his own. It's done me all right.'

'You can hardly set up on your own as a bus driver,' I pointed out, wondering why I was defending Norman when he'd just been so unpleasant to Hector, Kate and me.

'That's his problem,' said Saxon, gazing into the distance – or rather at the cupboard where Carol stored the cigarettes.

I glanced at his hands – strong and thickset, like his brother's – and noticed the yellow stains on the top joints of his forefinger and middle finger on both hands. I wondered whether being ambidextrous made him a more effective driving instructor, better able to judge the road whether in the driver's seat or the passenger's.

Although I didn't relish the prospect of spending an hour at a time in an enclosed space with this smoky, testy fellow, here was an opportunity to ask him directly about driving lessons. Maybe the prospect of an extra customer might tip the balance in favour of hiring his unfortunate brother to help with his business. At least that would divert Norman from the vacancy at Hector's House.

I stood back from the counter to chat to Saxon, having waved forward the lady between us to be served while we conversed.

'So, you're Saxon Arch,' I said, with a conciliatory smile. 'As in Succeed with Saxon?'

He wiggled his eyebrows suggestively. 'What if I am?'

'I'm interested in taking a few driving lessons.'

His demeanour transformed as if I'd waved a magic wand, his shoulders snapping back as if he were on parade. I wondered whether Norman was capable of such a quick change if we pressed the right button – or the wrong one, as had his manager at Highwayman.

'Of course, love, I'd be delighted,' Saxon was saying. 'When

Mrs Wetherley was unboxing a batch of scones and another of flapjacks, and judging by the banging and crashing from upstairs, Norman had started bright and early on the bookshelves.

Hector had turned the volume of his sound system up in an attempt to drown out the sound of hammering and sawing with Holst's *The Planets*, but even a full orchestra complete with pounding timpani were no match for Norman's toolkit.

After giving Hector a good-morning kiss, I slipped off my coat, and he took it from me to hang on its usual hook.

'What an awful racket!' I declared. 'Does putting up shelves really require so much hammering? My dad always uses a screwdriver and Rawlplugs. He never makes that much noise.'

Hector frowned. 'Yes, you're quite right, Sophie. A hammer and nails wouldn't provide as strong a connection with the wall. I've no idea why he's hammering. Would you mind holding the fort while I go up to check? Honestly, I can't take much more of this noise – he's been at it since seven o'clock this morning. Talk about keen. I had to get out of bed to let him in. Anyway, before I go, how are you this morning? And what's that heady smell? Are those carrier bags full of fermenting cider?'

He seemed in no hurry to confront Norman, perhaps for fear of what he might find, so I opened one of the carriers to allow him to peer inside.

'You're half right. They're full of fermenting apples. Maggie Burton's offloaded all her remaining crop on Carol, telling her to keep the proceeds of sales.'

'But you can't give windfalls away in the country at this time of year. You practically have to pay people to take them away.'

He prodded around in the bag, quickly withdrawing his hand when a dozy wasp surfaced, flying dreamily towards the

Sina shrieked. 'Oh, haven't you heard? Tommy's got a girl-friend in Slate Green now. He gets a later bus every day so he can go round to her house after school. He's stopped getting detentions too, as he'd rather go to hers.'

She flung her arms around herself and turned her back, running her hands up and down her skinny sides to suggest an embrace.

'Tommy and Stacey, sitting in a tree,' she sang, her young voice clear and reedy. 'K-I-S-S-I-N-G.'

Tommy grunted. 'We just do our homework together, that's all.'

Sina spun round again to face us. 'He's been getting better marks for his homework too. But you won't be able to do any of that once the bus service stops, Tommy. The council's going to put on a school minibus just for the big school kids, and you'll have to get that one straight after the end of the school day, or else stay at school all night.'

'They're not going to cancel the 27 if I have anything to do with it,' snapped Tommy. 'I'm going to fix that bus company once and for all.'

He grabbed his backpack and stormed out of the shop, sending the bookmarks flying again, and Sina helpfully gathered them up.

9

A SAXON INCURSION

Knowing that Hector would head to Clevedon as soon as we closed the shop, I had planned ahead how to make best use of my evening alone. I'd booked my first driving lesson with Saxon Arch at 6.30 p.m.

To calm my nerves about my appointment, I kept myself busy until the time Saxon was due to pick me up. I fed Blossom, cooked my tea and did a few household chores.

It was not the thought of getting behind the wheel of a different vehicle that made me nervous but spending time in an enclosed space with a strange man. I figured he was well enough known in the village that he ought to be safe enough. I also presumed he'd had to pass some kind of health and safety check to be allowed to run a driving school. Even so, it was with a fluttering heart that I said goodbye to Blossom when Saxon's red hatchback pulled up outside my house. I set her down on the deep front windowsill, and she watched me go out of the front door and down the garden path to the high street. I wondered who else in the village might notice me getting into Saxon's car.

As for my lesson with Hector, Saxon started out in the driver's seat.

'For your first lesson, I'll drive us to somewhere a little more secluded before teaching you the basics,' he informed me.

In silence, we headed out of the village and through a maze of lanes until, after several miles, we arrived at a large, empty car park on a small industrial estate. All the units seemed deserted, and some of the letters had fallen off the signboards, making the names of their former occupants staccato and edgy.

As Saxon applied the brake, I glanced at my watch. We were already nearly ten minutes into my hour-long lesson, and I had yet to touch the steering wheel. Was he taking advantage of my naivety, having me pay him to drive me about the countryside? At this rate, it would take far more lessons than it should for me to reach test standard, and it would cost a lot more too. Perhaps that was his plan.

We swapped seats, and he went through the ABC of the pedals routine. When he remarked how quickly I'd picked it up, I didn't tell him I'd already had a lesson with Hector. Before long, I was driving around the perimeter of the car park in third gear, slowing to turn a right-angled corner, then revving up again for the next stretch. By about the fifth circuit, Saxon appeared to have enough confidence in me to engage me in conversation, and I was starting to feel that learning to drive might not be so tricky after all.

'Do you have access to a car to practise with between lessons?' he asked, covering my left hand with his right as I made a too-noisy gear change.

I slid my hand out from under his as soon as I'd released the clutch.

'Well, there's Hector's Land Rover. He's happy to take me out in it if I want.'

I wasn't sure 'happy' was the right word, but it was more or less the truth.

'Still, I bet you'd rather learn with me.' He sat back, grinning, smug.

'What?' I took my eyes off the road – well, off the car park tarmac, at least – to stare at him, wondering what he was inferring.

He waved a hand airily. 'Oh, don't worry, darling, I can understand that. I mean, I know you need to keep in with your boss, but you must admit he's a bit of a drip. Poncey bookish type, my brother told me. I don't blame you for locking onto me in the shop the other day. And I know it's not a problem for you to find the necessary readies for lessons, what with being your batty old auntie's heiress, and all. But you know...'

His right hand bypassed the gear stick and landed on my left thigh. 'There are other ways of paying, if you get my drift.'

Instinctively, I let go of the steering wheel to slap his straying hand. 'How dare you!'

He recoiled as if at an explosion.

'You bring me out here and insult my boyfriend, besmirch the memory of my lovely great aunt, and then lay your grubby hands on me! That's nothing short of assault.'

I steered the car towards the car park's exit sign.

'I've had enough of this. I'm driving us straight home now.' I swung the car onto the lane, taking only a small piece of hedgerow with us. As we headed through the winding lanes in second gear, I ignored Saxon's sharp intakes of breath. I wasn't entirely confident about changing gears yet and thought it better to stick with the gear I knew best.

'If you think you're getting any more business from me, you've got another think coming,' I stormed, steering abruptly into a layby to let a tractor pass. 'And I'm not paying for this lesson either, as I'll have had barely twenty minutes behind the wheel by the time I get home.'

Saxon, wide-eyed, was gripping the dashboard with both hands now. At least that meant he was keeping them away from me. But he hadn't given up yet.

'Listen, darling, if it's professional driving lessons you're after, I'm the only person you'll get them from in Wendlebury. The instructors in Slate Green won't come out this far, any more than taxi drivers will. It takes too long to drive here and back. It's not worth their while. So, you're stuck with me, babe, and you'd better get used to the idea, especially once the buses pack up.'

'Nonsense. I'll just take one of those crash courses instead – you know, the sort where they teach you to pass your test in a week.' Only as I spoke did I seriously consider that as a viable alternative. At least it should get it over with quickly. 'And don't call me *babe*.'

'They don't call them crash courses for nothing,' he retorted.

The lane had widened a little, but still not enough to allow two-way traffic. An elderly man in a green saloon was approaching us, and I slowed down, steering into a passing place just ahead. The old man hesitated.

'Oh, come on, love, you can get a bus through there!' I shouted, beckoning him to advance.

'Sophie, I really don't think...'

Saxon's voice petered out as the saloon edged towards us. All smiles now, I raised my palm to thank him. Only our wing mirrors made contact. I counted that as a win. For the rest of the journey home, Saxon had his hands over his eyes, uncovering them only when I drew to a halt in front of the 'Wendlebury Barrow Welcomes Careful Drivers' sign.

'I'll walk the rest of the way from here, thank you,' I declared, getting out and slamming the door behind me.

By the time I got home, my heart was pounding. When I caught sight of my face in the wall mirror, my cheeks were aflame. Filling the kettle for a calming cup of tea made me notice my hands were shaking. Only then did I realise just how upsetting the abortive lesson had been – and how dangerous, in more ways than one.

The sign at the village boundary had never looked so good. Remembering its slogan, I burst out laughing. Careful drivers? Perhaps the village wouldn't truly welcome a driver like me until I'd had a bit more practice.

But as I slumped down onto the sofa with my mug of tea, and Blossom jumped onto my lap, it occurred to me that in the space of a day, Hector and I had made enemies of both the Arch brothers.

10

ON THE WARPATH

I was glad to have the impending parish council emergency meeting to think about to prevent me dwelling on the travesty of my driving lesson with Saxon Arch. Only now did it dawn on me how reckless I had been to drive all the way from the industrial estate to the village without prior experience of driving on actual roads. Why hadn't Saxon stopped me? Perhaps he'd thought it was riskier to interfere when I was in such an indignant mood than to let me keep going. How far would he have let me continue without intervening? Until the car ran out of petrol? The man was a coward and an idiot, as well as a lecher and a bully.

By the time Hector called in to my cottage on his way home from Clevedon, I'd calmed down a little, with the help of a purging shower, and changed into my comforting kitten onesie. When Hector let himself in, I was immersed in an escapist novel, curled up on the ancient chintz sofa beside the wood-burner.

Full of inconsequential news from his parents, Hector didn't think to ask me how my evening had gone, much to my relief. I

front of the shop. I pulled *The Weekly Slate* from my satchel to waft the wasp out of the door and into the street.

'I told Carol your mum wanted them for her freezer,' I explained, straightening out the newspaper.

Hector raised his eyebrows. 'Do you think she will?'

'Not really but buying them helped Carol. She sends your mum and dad her love.'

Hector settled back again on his stool. 'Oh well, if it helps Carol out.'

A mischievous thought occurred to me. 'Although maybe she should be subsidising the bookshop, seeing the size of the diamond engagement ring Ted's just given her. It's massive!'

'Really? How did he afford that? I hope he didn't take out a loan. Besides, I would have expected Carol to choose a modest ring. She doesn't usually go in for bling.'

'Oh, she didn't get any say in the matter. Ted chose it and bought it by himself. She just had to give him her ring size.'

Mrs Wetherley, her unpacking finished, came to join us.

'Carol's a lucky lady,' she said. 'Ted must have paid thousands for it. You should see it, Hector!' She set her receipt for the morning's delivery on the counter. 'Goodness knows she's waited long enough for a decent fellow to come along. I, for one, don't begrudge her such a chunky token of his affection.'

Hector opened the till and paid her in cash.

'See you in the morning,' she said brightly, scooping it up, before following in the wake of the wasp, only without the need for a rolled-up newspaper to shoo her on her way.

Hector waited until the door had closed behind Mrs Wetherley before bursting out laughing.

'Oh, you innocents! I bet it's not real. Where would Ted get the money to buy a genuine huge diamond? It's probably just a cubic zirconia. They're a fraction of the price, and to the uncul-

expect he presumed I'd spent the entire evening reading. I wasn't about to disillusion him. As far as I was concerned, my driving lesson with Saxon Arch never happened.

* * *

The next evening, the parish council meeting was due to start in the village hall at 7.30 p.m., with a private session for council members for half an hour before that. After a light supper at his flat, surrounded by boxes of second-hand books and planks waiting to be turned into shelves, Hector and I strolled over to the village hall at about 7.20 p.m. By this time, a long and noisy queue had already formed, despite the damp autumn air and thin, chilly mist shrouding the playing field beside the hall.

Only at 7.30 p.m. were parishioners allowed to enter the hall. They always arrived at village events eager and early, whether a school play, a jumble sale, a wedding or a funeral.

At the front of the queue was an enthusiastic crowd of pensioners clutching their free bus passes, ready to wave them in protest at the visitor from Highwayman. Several of them had made placards, with slogans such as 'Don't Take Away Our Freedom' and 'Pensioners' Rights' and 'Cross Us at Your Peril'.

Next in the queue was a group of secondary school pupils who took the number 27 to and from the school in Slate Green every day. Four teenage girls had kitted themselves out as cheerleaders and were earnestly rehearsing their routine: a carefully choreographed number to a jingle that began, 'Listen up, you Highwayman', and which culminated in their flipping over cardboard signs to reveal the message 'SOBS: Save Our Bus Service' (with a weeping emoji).

Many people had brought whistles and improvised percussion instruments, such as saucepan lids and wooden spoons, to add volume to their protests.

One middle-aged lady, Beryl Robertson, had even brought her own soapbox to stand on. Her rainbow-striped jumpsuit and scarlet top hat would have drawn attention without the added height.

Beryl was a frequent customer at Hector's House, often ordering thick textbooks on climate science and environmental tracts. She was very well informed.

'Good evening, Beryl,' said Hector affably, as we walked past her towards the end of the queue.

Her unexpected reply stopped us in our tracks. 'Please call me Norma.'

'Sorry, I thought you were Beryl Robertson. You must get this all the time. You are exactly like Beryl.'

An identical twin himself, Hector had jumped to a reasonable conclusion.

Not-Beryl stepped down from her soapbox. Even with the hat, she was now shorter than me, and much shorter than Hector.

'No, Hector, I *am* Beryl, or rather, I was, until last week, when I changed my name by deed poll to "No More Cuts" in protest.' She spelled the three words out. 'The "No-More" is hyphenated. But unfortunately, everyone's calling me Norma.'

Hector shrugged. 'Okay, then. Good evening, Norma.'

'Don't "good evening" me, Hector Munro,' came a gruff voice behind her, and I jumped at the sight of Norman Arch, decked out in his former bus driver's uniform. I was surprised that Highwayman hadn't made him give it back when they sacked him, like a dishonourably discharged soldier being stripped of his rank insignia. I suppose it wasn't as if Highwayman was going to replace him. The current driver of the 27 was providing temporary cover until the service was withdrawn.

Beryl – I mean, Norma – jumped back on her box to look the stocky Mr Arch in the eye. 'Don't be such a chump, Norman. Hector was talking to me. No need for you to be rude to him. You don't have a monopoly on the name.'

Norman scowled. 'No, but it could cause confusion.'

'Nonsense,' retorted Norma. 'No-More is very different from Norman, in sound and meaning. I don't think anyone's going to confuse the two of us. It's not as if we look alike.'

As Norma and Norman continued to squabble, Hector tugged at my hand to keep walking. We joined the back of the queue, where Billy was shuffling about, passing a huge pair of decorator's scissors from hand to hand, to which he'd affixed the side of a cardboard Weetabix carton. On its blank back, he'd written 'Don't be a Beeching'.

Beside him, Tommy was puzzling of its meaning.

'Dr Beeching was the first chairman of the British Railways Board,' explained Billy. 'And what did he do? Cut lines and closed stations.'

The sound of an air-horn at the centre of the car park cut Billy short, sparing Tommy a further history lesson. Norma had set down her soap box where everyone in the queue could see her and had sounded the horn to attract the crowd's attention for her address. With her free hand, she raised a megaphone to her lips.

'Wendlebury Barrow, unite!' she cried. 'Let us work together to prevent the axing of our precious bus service, because you can be sure once we lose it, it's never coming back. I beseech you all to use it all you can between now and its supposed abolition – because if we show just how much we need it, they dare not take it away.'

'I wouldn't be too sure,' came a voice from halfway down the queue. 'They'll do what they like, regardless. Highwayman doesn't care for the little people like us.'

There were cries of 'shame!' and 'hear, hear' along the queue.

Thus encouraged, Norma continued.

'If you've abandoned the bus for a car since the price hike last year, consider using the bus for the next few weeks to show solidarity. If you've a bus pass, take as many trips as you can. That'll show how much we need the service.'

'She's right, you know,' Norman Arch called out. They must have resolved their differences quickly. 'The bus company takes notice of passenger statistics.'

Maggie Burton waved her hand in the air like an eager child in the classroom. 'But surely, it's too late now? They've made their decision.'

'While the number 27 is still running, there's a chance they might re-engage,' said Norma through the loudspeaker. 'If there wasn't any hope, they wouldn't have called this meeting.'

'Don't you believe it!' came a cry from towards the front of the queue. 'It's a sham.'

'This meeting is just to make us feel we've been consulted,' said their companion. 'Then they'll do whatever they were going to do anyway.'

Just then a car horn sounded at the entrance to the car park as a BBC Cotswolds car turned in and began to edge its way across to a parking space. A ripple of 'oohs' and 'aahs' ran along the queue. Several people started to tidy their hair and check their make-up in hope of appearing on the local television news.

The media types were cutting their arrival fine, as at that moment, the doors to the village hall opened and everyone hurried inside, those at the front of the queue almost running to get the best seats.

Hector and I followed at a more leisurely pace.

'I wonder whether this Highwayman fellow knows what he's up against,' said Hector as we passed through the door at last. 'He might have the final yea or nay about the 27 bus, but Wendlebury Barrow will give him a run for his money. Just about everyone who's anyone in the village is here. We've turned out in force.'

'Yes,' I said, thinking to myself... *Everyone except Saxon Arch.*

mechanical faults developing for no apparent reason over the last year, our running repair costs have trebled.'

'But your buses are built like tanks,' said Norma, raising her hand only after he'd started speaking. 'They don't usually sustain so much wear and tear. Sounds to me like someone's been sabotaging it. I heard someone's been stitching you up. Maybe it's a dirty tricks campaign by one of your rivals?'

Leif spluttered slightly. Whether a laugh or a gasp, it was hard to tell.

'I'm sorry, but I couldn't possibly comment on the practices of our competition. Innocent until proven guilty. One must presume Highwayman has just been very unfortunate lately. All the more reason to focus on the development of a new, more sustainable service. But that's going to take time as well as money.

'I'm sure you'll agree that even the most perfect gas lamp has no place in the modern home.' He waited, scanning the audience again, before continuing. 'Which is why we at Highwayman are standing down our diesel buses with a view to replacing them with electric vehicles powered by renewable energy. I'm sure you've all heard of the famous Number 2 bus in Bristol, so-called because it's powered by human effluent.'

'That means poo,' Billy said loudly, for Tommy's benefit.

The schoolchildren in the hall sniggered.

'We are also looking at new driver configurations,' continued Leif Oakham.

'Is that like yoga?' called a wag.

If Leif Oakham heard, he did not mind. 'The good news is, long term, we hope to introduce such new sustainable systems to rural constituencies like Wendlebury Barrow by 2030. On the downside, in the meantime we have no choice but to withdraw the current service until such time as—'

Before he could finish his sentence, a roar went up from the audience.

'That's no good to us!'

'We need buses now!'

'Don't you believe him – when it's gone, it's gone. They'll never bring it back.'

'Just like the Beeching Cuts were for our train station. It'll be gone for ever.'

'You don't care about villages at all!'

Michael Greenaway leaped to his feet and raised his hands for silence. 'One at a time, please! And please give Mr Oakham a chance to respond to your questions. Please raise your hands if you have a sensible question or comment – and please do each other the courtesy of listening.'

To Michael Greenaway's obvious relief, the shouting subsided, then dozens of hands went up. Unfortunately, although Leif Oakham patiently answered every question, it seemed Highwayman's decision to scrap the 27 bus was final.

'If only the 27 bus was full every day, it might be a different matter,' he conceded. 'But with so many of our regular passengers travelling on free passes, at current fuel prices, we make a loss on almost every trip, and that's without factoring in the drivers' wages.'

'Ha! We know what you do about the drivers.' This was Norman Arch, on his feet and raising a fist. 'You sack 'em on trumped-up charges so you don't have to fork out redundancy.'

Kate, on stage as a member of the parish council, raised her hand to speak. 'Mr Oakham, on Mr Arch's behalf, it seems unfair to have dismissed him for supposed gross misconduct, when all he was doing was enforcing company rules against passengers eating and drinking on board his bus.'

Leif Oakham turned to address Kate. 'Councillor Barker, I'm

afraid now isn't the time or place to discuss human resources issues. Besides, the tribunal has already reached its final conclusion.'

Norma stood up, shaking a fist. 'What she says is true, though.'

'I've a right to eat,' came a woman's voice from near the front. Mrs Boggins got to her feet and turned to address Norman Arch a few rows behind her. She may have been small and thin, but her voice and her vigour were outsized. 'I'm medically exempt. It's me glands. You let Frank Marchant's blind dog on the bus. You gotta let me eat, else I might faint. Besides, I'd got a bag of doughnuts reduced for quick sale at the bakers', so I had to eat them quick before they went off.'

As a ripple of laughter went round the room, Kate gave a slight shake of the head to Leif Oakham to contradict Janice Boggins' claim to special circumstances.

'Mr Marchant's guide dog is hardly an equivalent to a bag of cut-priced doughnuts,' said Kate, clearly struggling to keep a straight face.

'Oh yes, and a sticky bun helped me across the road this morning,' shouted a joker from the back, and everyone except Mrs Boggins laughed.

Michael Greenaway raised his hands again for silence. 'I fear we're veering away from the purpose of this meeting now and becoming unpleasantly personal. Mr Oakham, is there perhaps anything else you'd like to tell the audience?'

'Greenaway's been primed,' murmured Hector. 'It's as if Leif Oakham's PR has given him a script.'

Leif Oakham brightened. 'I predict a mix of non-polluting biodiesel vehicles and electric motors,' he began.

'What, like milk floats?' called Billy. 'Those would take hours to get to Slate Green.'

'Keep up with the times, Bill,' a member of the audience called out before Leif Oakham could reply. 'Electric cars have got real welly now.'

Leif Oakham smiled, clearly more comfortable on this topic. 'Indeed, I can tell you from personal experience that modern electric vehicles provide a smooth, swift and near-silent ride.'

'They do sound like milk floats, though,' added the previous commenter.

'Councillor Barker here was regaling me earlier with her own experience of an electric bicycle,' Leif Oakham continued.

He gave Kate an old-fashioned bow, and Kate smiled politely, though I sensed that inside she was cringing.

'Not everyone can afford electric bikes and cars, Mr Oakham,' Kate put in, anticipating what the audience's next objection might be.

'Not all of us could manage to stay upright on a bike, electric or not,' added an elderly lady halfway back. 'Though I wouldn't say no to an electric tricycle if someone else paid for it.'

'I'd like an electric tricycle,' said Tommy. 'I'd get it turbocharged.'

The audience quickly fell to talking amongst itself, speculating on other unlikely solutions to our dilemma.

Michael Greenaway tapped his microphone for everyone's attention. 'Ladies and gentlemen, boys and girls, I think we've finished the serious business for the evening, so I vote we close the meeting.'

'Seconded!' several of his fellow councillors were quick to agree. The stage curtains closed, hiding them from our view. Then the house lights went up, and a hall committee member propped open the double doors to hasten our exit.

'I could've told you we shouldn't trust a man with a daft

name like Leif,' grumbled Billy, getting up from his seat on the ladder.

'You wouldn't say that about Leif Erikson,' retorted Tommy.

'Who's he, the boss of one of them mobile phone companies?' said Billy.

Hector and I laughed.

'No, he was a great explorer,' explained Tommy. 'We've been doing him at school in American history. He got to America before Christopher Columbus, and he started out in Iceland.'

'Oh, a pesky Viking.' Billy tutted. 'Well, you know what trouble they were.'

When we crossed the car park, Leif Oakham emerged from the stage door at the back of the hall, avoiding the crowd of the villagers, and he climbed into the back seat of a sleek black Tesla that had been waiting for him.

'Not only does the Viking have an electric car, but he's got a chauffeur too,' Hector observed. 'I wonder when he last travelled anywhere by bus?'

As the crowd surged into the high street, with us in their midst, I resolved to book myself on an intensive driving course as soon as I could find one.

12

ON THE OFFENSIVE

If Leif Oakham thought he'd subdued local protests with his smooth talking, he was very much mistaken, as Hector and I discovered when we called in for a drink at The Bluebird after the meeting had finished. All anyone could talk of was rebellion and protest.

'Supposing I threw a bucket of water over that Twiggy's electric car?' Billy was saying as he stood at the bar, tankard in hand. 'Would that kill 'im or just give him an electric shock?'

Stan the publican laughed. 'Sorry, Bill, you'd just be giving him a free carwash. How do you think they'd ever drive anywhere in the rain if they couldn't get wet? It's not like throwing a toaster in his bath.'

I shuddered. 'What an awful thought, Stan! Surely there are more peaceful ways to make our point. How about if we all wrote to our MP?'

Stan gave a hollow laugh. 'Last time I heard, he was on holiday in the Maldives. I don't think he gives two hoots about the likes of us.'

'Okay, letter-writing to other people then. To the county council, for a start. Or a social media campaign.'

'What we want is physical action,' said Norma Cuts. 'Something tangible and hard to ignore. So much of social media is just sharing videos with people who agree with you. It's either an echo chamber or a nasty pit of trolls. Not the place to get something done at a local level.'

'Actually, I think the solution is simple,' said Kate. 'We should show how much we need the bus in the most obvious way – by travelling on it as much as possible in its remaining time. Anyone with a free bus pass should spend as much time on it as they can to make the bus look full.'

'That's exactly what I was saying just now, when you were all hidden away behind the stage curtain!' cried Norma, sounding triumphant.

'I don't mind doing my shopping by bus for a change,' said one of the school-run mums. 'I hate parking in that multi-storey, anyway.'

'I could take the littl'uns for a day out at the weekend,' said one of the dads. 'They think it's fun riding on the bus. They'll change their minds once they go up to big school and must take the bus every day. The novelty will soon wear off. If it's still running, that is.'

His glum expression told me he was picturing having to drive them back and forth every day himself.

'Apparently the council is required by law to provide transport to take every child to their nearest secondary school,' said the chair of the village school PTA, who had a teenager already at Slate Green Secondary School. 'In the absence of a public bus, they'll just have to buy a minibus and hire a driver themselves.'

'If they do that, you can bet the service will be the bare minimum,' said the dad. 'Just one bus; morning and afternoon. Our poor kids won't be able to stay late for sports or after-school clubs unless their parents can pick them up.'

'That's just what Sina was telling us earlier,' said Hector gloomily, as we weaved our way through the crowd at the bar towards an empty bench seat in the corner. 'So it looks like Tommy's new-found love-life is scuppered.'

I took a sip of my white wine, cool and refreshing after the stuffy village hall.

'Poor Tommy. And not only for romantic reasons. That Stacey's a good influence on his study habits. Fancy Tommy knowing more than Billy about history!'

Hector raised his pint glass in tribute to her before taking a hearty swig. 'So, Sophie, what are you going to do to help the cause? Chain yourself to the bus stop? Chain me to the bus stop?'

I laughed. 'I thought I'd take Kate's advice and catch the bus tomorrow to do your banking. It'll save you taking the Land Rover out.'

I'd rather have been chauffeured by Hector, but catching the bus for once seemed the least I could do to support the campaign.

13

THE WHEELS ON THE BUS

The next morning, after popping in briefly to the village shop, I crossed the road to the bus stop. The queue was shorter than I'd expected from the fighting talk in The Bluebird the night before. Admittedly, this wasn't the first bus of the day, which took the older village children to Slate Green Secondary School and the nine-to-five workers to their jobs, so it wasn't going to be at its busiest. But I had expected more passengers – those people who didn't use it to go to work but wanted to demonstrate to High-wayman the need for our bus service. And where were all the pensioners with free bus passes? From what she'd said, I'd expected to see Maggie Burton there at least, but as I arrived, she was walking away from the bus stop.

In fact, there were so few people waiting for the bus that you could barely call it a queue. Janice Boggins was at the front, almost as if defying anyone to queue-jump, touching the bus stop sign as if claiming her territory. In her other hand, she was carrying a small picnic hamper with a red, white and blue gingham bow on the handle. I guessed she'd packed enough food to keep her going all day. I didn't like her for what she'd done to Norman, but at least she was helping to save the bus service.

Standing a couple of feet behind her was Beryl – I mean, Norma Cuts. I could hardly have missed her. She was wearing a fluorescent orange T-shirt with her new name on it and holding a hand-painted placard that read, 'Stand and deliver the 27 bus', beside a drawing of a cartoon Dick Turpin figure wielding a pistol in each hand. I hoped that was the closest to violence the campaign would see.

Loitering in the bus shelter and disregarding the pair of them was Norman Arch, chewing gum with his mouth open and pretending to be engrossed in a tabloid newspaper, but his eyes weren't moving, so he wasn't really reading it. Perhaps he was just looking at the pictures or concentrating on solving the chess problem. I thought the latter unlikely.

'Morning, Mrs Boggins, Norma, Norman,' I greeted them cheerfully. It was customary in Wendlebury to say hello to anyone you passed in the street, whether or not you recognised them. I once had an old university friend to stay who had only ever lived in cities. One morning she returned from a solo walk to the village shop astonished. 'How did everybody know me?' she asked and wondered why I fell about laughing.

Janice and Norma returned my greeting, but Norman didn't stir. Either he was embarrassed by the poor job he'd made of the bookshop shelves, or he was angry with me because he associated me with Hector. He must have seen Hector as the villain of the piece for sacking him part way through the job.

There again, he might feel awkward that I'd caught him out after telling me he had no money to catch the bus into town to sign on every other Tuesday. Yet here he was about to climb aboard on a Friday. What was he up to?

Before I'd had a chance to do more than compliment Norma

Cuts on her eye-catching placard, the bus came trundling along the high street and pulled up at the bus stop. I didn't have to wait long to board. Janice and Norma had their free senior citizens' bus passes at the ready for the driver to scan, and Norman and I both had the right change for our fares.

There must have been no love lost between Norman and his replacement, so I was not surprised when they didn't speak to each other. Norman must also have found it humiliating to have to pay a fare rather than using the free staff pass he'd been entitled to previously. Every journey must have been a fresh reminder of his dismissal.

I would have felt rude saying nothing as I climbed aboard, so I greeted the driver with a cheery 'Good morning!' He made no comment in return, just sat with a glazed expression silently chomping on bubble gum. At least he kept his mouth closed.

Janice headed for her favourite seat – the one beside the luggage rack at the front, just behind the driver. It's slightly higher than the rest of the downstairs seats, and a single, unlike the others. It rather reminds me a throne. I'd often seen Janice sail past the bookshop sitting there, and I half expected her to give a royal wave.

Beryl chose the first double seat, halfway down the bus, just behind the exit doors. She positioned her placard against the window so that anyone the bus passed might see it. If, like Janice, she was planning to stay on the bus all day in protest, she was going to have a dull time with no view, but presumably she was happy to make that sacrifice for the cause.

Norman stomped down to the back of the bus, as far as it was possible to be from the rest of us, snagging the scruffy brown holdall he was carrying on the edge of every seat – bump, bump, bump – as he went. By the time I had paid my fare, he was hiding behind his newspaper once more.

Norma gave me such a broad smile as I made my way down the aisle that I felt compelled to sit on the double seat across the aisle from hers. In an almost empty bus with so many empty double seats, it would have felt intrusive to sit right next to her. Instead, I resigned myself to a loud conversation across the aisle as we shouted to be heard above the chug of the diesel engine.

Janice ignored us all, opening her picnic basket and examining the contents as if doing a stock-take and planning how to make the contents last all day. Or perhaps she too was making an excuse not to look at Norma and me. After all, she must have packed the basket herself that morning, so she must have known what was in there.

To my surprise, I found it a refreshing change to take the bus. While Norma explained at great length how and why the world should stop using fossil fuels immediately and what we should use instead, I enjoyed the autumnal scenery, stubbly brown fields and copper-leaved trees dark against the cool, bright morning light. The morning mist had not quite burned off, leaving every colour enriched by residual dampness.

The bus picked up a handful of additional passengers along the way, and all but Janice and Norma got off at the bus station by the shopping centre.

With my satchel slung across my body, I marched briskly to the bank, eager to be relieved of the responsibility of carrying so much cash. At least it wasn't heavy, consisting mostly of notes – we usually bagged up our small change and swapped it for bank notes with Stan at The Bluebird or Carol at the village shop, as with no bank in our village, they were always short of coins – so no one could tell the value of my load. All the same, I was glad to hand it over to the counter clerk at the bank.

With an hour to kill before the return bus – during which Norma and Janice would have made a round trip – I dawdled over a couple of other errands for the shop, buying staples and Sellotape from the stationer's and a catering pack of paper servi-ettes from the budget supermarket.

Then I treated myself to a hot chocolate from a coffee shop and sat at a pavement table, drawing my scarf about my neck to keep out the chill, and spent a pleasant half-hour people-watch-ing. I wondered whether I might bump into Norman again or spot him going about his daily business. I was rather relieved that I didn't.

When I finally clambered aboard the bus for the journey home, Janice was, as expected, still in her favourite seat, supping the contents of one of those highly expensive cans of coffee, the sort that warm up when you pull a tab and shake them. That didn't strike me as her usual fare. I wondered why she hadn't made a flask of hot coffee instead. It would have been much cheaper. To be fair, I had just splashed out on a hot chocolate I didn't really need, so I was being hypocritical to begrudge her a fancy drink herself. Besides, I had no reason to think she was short of money.

Norma was also still in the same seat, pink-cheeked with excitement as she peered round the edge of her placard to acknowledge the shouts and waves of support from passers-by. I hadn't appreciated until then the fellow-feeling from passengers on other routes, but they must have been worried that if our bus could be axed, theirs might be next to go.

'Well done, Norma,' I said as I settled my bag of shopping on the spare seat beside me. 'You're really raising awareness. Are you planning to travel round on the bus all day?'

She shot a guilty glance at Janice and lowered her voice. I had to lean across the aisle to hear her answer as the bus moved off from its stand.

'I'm planning to get off at the shopping centre next time

around for a comfort break. Then I'll do another round trip, followed by the single journey home. I think that's long enough for me for one day. But I'll carry on campaigning once I get home. I'll be blogging about my day to spread the word.'

I pointed out of the window to where a teenager was snapping her, and Norma immediately pulled a grim face for effect, followed by a cheery smile of thanks.

'Hurrah, that'll be one for the TikTok generation,' she said. Then she held out her phone to me. 'Would you mind taking a picture of me that I can use as an illustration on my blog?'

'Sure.'

I took a few as she presented herself in various poses by her placard, giving an impressive repertoire of facial expressions from grief-stricken to incensed. I passed the phone back to her across the aisle.

'You weren't tempted to bring a picnic to while away the day?' I asked her. I shot a mischievous side-eye at Janice, who was now making headway with a little gauze bag of sugared almonds, the kind they give as wedding favours in Italy. Full marks to her for picnicking in style.

Norma raised her eyebrows at the sign forbidding food and drink on board, which was immediately above Janice's head.

'No, I'll grab a vegan sausage roll from Greggs when I get off for my comfort break,' replied Norma, mouthing those last few words for confidentiality. 'I wonder whether Janice will get off for a trip to the ladies' too. If not, you have to admire the strength of her bladder if she can stay on board all day long without spending a penny.'

Then she returned her attention to her placard, making the most of the opportunity to catch the attention of drivers on the busy main road.

14

ROUND AND ROUND

Janice did need to step off the bus late afternoon, making a quick dash to the public toilets in the bus station before the 4.30 p.m. bus departed. Although I'd been back at the bookshop since early afternoon, I knew this because Tommy regaled me on the stand-off he'd had with her over her favourite seat when he dashed onto the bus at the terminus in her absence. When he bowled into Hector's House just after five, he was still incensed that she'd routed him.

'But I thought kids usually like to sit at the back of the bus?' I queried. 'I know I did when I was your age. On our school bus, it was a rite of passage to reach the top of the pecking order that allowed you to sit on the bench across the back!'

It seemed that hadn't changed.

'Yes, but this time I particularly wanted to sit there for my protest, because I know the driver can't see that seat as well as he can the back seat.'

'Don't tell me you'd brought a picnic too?' Tommy was permanently peckish, but, like Janice, he carried not a gram of spare fat on his slender frame.

'Oh no, it's nothing to do with food.' He glanced around the tearoom hopefully. 'Although I could manage a biscuit if you've got any broken ones you were about to throw away?'

I lifted the clear plastic dome over the single remaining slice of chocolate cake. It would be too dry to serve next day, I told myself, although it wasn't true. When he picked it up with his right hand, I slipped a plate underneath to catch the crumbs, but he refused to take it, keeping his left hand in his school blazer pocket.

'No, what I was going to do was superglue myself to the seat. That was going to be my big protest. Well, one of them, anyway. So, I'd just spread the little tube all over that seat and was about to sit on it when Mrs Boggins barged up and shoved me out of the way with her soppy little basket. I really tried to stop her from sitting down, but I couldn't. She just pushed me out of the way. Then more passengers were getting on and telling me to move along, so I went to sit at the back instead. So, she'll have got stuck to the seat rather than me. Oh, well.' He shrugged. 'I suppose that still counts as a protest. It's just her doing it instead of me.'

I bit my lip to hide my smile. 'I probably shouldn't say this, Tommy, but I think it serves her right for being so rude to you. Just as well she was wearing a long, thick skirt. At least it'll only be her clothes that stick to the seat rather than her legs. Superglue bonds skin in seconds.'

'Don't I know it,' he grumbled, pulling his left hand out of his pocket at last, revealing the flattened tube of superglue adhered firmly to his thumb and index finger. He held his hand up with the tube hanging down, but even gravity didn't make it drop off. 'I know you're meant to wash it off straight away with washing-up liquid if it gets on your skin, but I could hardly do that on the bus.'

I got the impression this was not the first time he'd accidentally superglued himself.

I waved him round to the handbasin behind the tearoom counter and filled it with warm, soapy water. Then I took the cake from him and put it on the plate.

'There, soak your hand for as long as it takes to prise the tube off your skin. The cake will still be waiting for you when you're done.'

I started to wipe down the counter, still chatting to Tommy. 'So, what happened when your bus got back to Wendlebury? Did Mrs Boggins try to get off and discover that she couldn't?'

'No. I jumped off the bus first – I didn't want a ticking-off from Old Bogroll. Then that Norma lady got off with her big sign. But Bogroll just stayed on. Didn't even look at me as the bus doors closed and it pulled away. Pretty lucky, actually. As the bus pulled away, I realised she was fast asleep. Buses and cars do that to people sometimes. My little sister always used to fall asleep in my dad's car when she was a baby. When she wouldn't stop crying, he used to take her out for drives, and only bring her back asleep.'

Tommy looked wistful. He seldom talked about his father, who had left when he was very young.

'How are your fingers now?' I asked to distract him.

With the showmanship of a conjuror producing a rabbit from a hat, he whipped his hand out of the handbasin, sending a soapy tidal wave onto the floor. The empty glue tube remained floating on the surface of the remaining water, and he stretched his fingers apart, like a pianist checking his span.

'Thanks, Sophie. Have you got any more cake?'

15

FIRESTARTER

It was my turn to cook dinner for Hector. Since we'd come back from Scotland, we had fallen into the habit of alternating, apart from earlier in the week when he'd dined with his mum and dad. We agreed he'd stroll down to my cottage around seven, to allow him an hour of uninterrupted work on *The Kiss of the Sun*. He liked using May's old writing bureau that stood in the corner of my little front room. Although it was on the small side for him, I think he took inspiration from the fact that she'd penned so many of her bestselling travel books there.

Hector usually squeezed in at least one writing sprint during the shop's opening hours, but if we had no other plans of an evening, he'd often put in an hour between closing time and dinner. He espoused Graham Greene's principle of aiming for five hundred words a day, which had enabled him to finish quite a few books now, which he self-published under the pseudonym Hermione Minty.

In the meantime, I'd wound down nicely, making a fuss of Blossom before browning some chicken pieces in the frying pan and setting them to roast on a bed of vegetables in the oven.

Now that the nights were drawing in, we both appreciated hearty, hot evening meals.

I was just putting a match to the wigwam of paper and kindling inside the wood-burner when there was a frantic knocking at the door. I closed the little cast-iron door before peeking through a chink in the curtains to see who was making such a fuss.

To my surprise, it was Hector, wide-eyed and restless on the step, spotlit by the street lamp amid a swirling pool of mist. I went to let him in.

'Have you lost your key, you silly—'

My voice petered out when I saw his pallor. I grabbed his arm and drew him inside, closing the door behind him.

'Hector, whatever's the matter? You look like you've seen a ghost.'

I steered him over to the sofa and he almost fell rather than sat down. I knelt in front of him, taking his cold hands in my warm ones.

'Near as damn it,' he replied, his voice hoarse. I blamed the chilly evening air. 'I just saw Bob.'

Bob was a police officer who lived in the village and worked from the police station in Slate Green. The days of Wendlebury having its own bobby were long gone, although my elderly neighbour, Joshua, liked to regale me with stories of the one that had kept local reprobates in check when he was a boy.

'Bob? He's not exactly scary.'

My first encounter with Bob was when he was in fancy dress as a Keystone Cop at the Village Show. I'd found it hard to take him seriously after that.

'No, but what he told me came as a shock.'

He put his hands on my shoulders and gazed into my eyes.

'When I saw him, he was just coming away from the

Bogginses' cottage on the High Street. I thought he was looking a bit shaky, so I asked him if he was okay. He said, no, not really, he'd just delivered a message on behalf of the family liaison officer based at Slate Green. It was Mr Boggins.'

My hand shot to my mouth. 'Oh no, has poor Mr Boggins been in a car accident?'

Mr Boggins was one of the villagers who had started driving to work when the bus fare doubled. How cruel if he had lost his life because of the price rise. If so, I hoped Leif Oakham and his greedy shareholders would lose sleep over their decision.

The kindling began to crackle.

'No, it wasn't about Mr Boggins. He'd had to go and speak to Mr Boggins. It was Mrs Boggins, Janice, who was the problem.'

'Janice?' I got to my feet and fetched an open bottle of red wine that I'd set by the cooker to warm. Two glasses were already on the coffee table.

'Ah yes, poor Janice!' I said with a wry smile as I returned. 'Didn't you hear Tommy telling me earlier how he'd accidentally superglued her to the seat of the bus? Never mind, I expect she'll live.'

Hector grabbed my free hand with such force that a few drops of wine splashed out of the bottle and onto the hearth, leaving marks the colour of blood.

'No, she won't. She's not just superglued. She'd dead.'

I nearly dropped the bottle. 'Dead? But where? How?'

Hector's left eyebrow twitched. 'On the bus. The driver found her slumped in her seat once he'd parked for the night in the depot at the end of his shift. At first, he assumed she was making a token protest against the service cuts by refusing to get off. Then he thought she was asleep. When he gave her a shake to wake her up, she just keeled over. Well, not all the way over onto the floor, because her bottom was stuck fast to her seat.'

'That'll be Tommy's superglue. My goodness, do you think she somehow ingested some of it? Has Tommy poisoned her? Not on purpose, of course, but how will it look for him if...'

I couldn't bear to continue. I had just realised I must have been one of the last people to see her alive. What had her last words been? Hopefully not the abuse she'd hurled at Tommy when defending her favourite seat.

'I suppose there'll be a post-mortem unless she was under the doctor for something,' said Hector. 'We all thought she was hale and hearty, but perhaps there was an underlying condition that caused her to die on the bus. We'll just have to wait for the post-mortem results to find out.'

'That will take weeks, won't it?' I asked.

Hector shook his head. 'Apparently, they're going to rush it through. Bob said that when they suspect foul play, they do what's called a special post-mortem, usually within the next twenty-four hours or so.'

A draught down the chimney caused the pyramid of kindling to shift sideways in the wood-burner, sending a fierce flame roaring against the stove doors and rattling the glass panels like the bones of a skeleton on Halloween.

16

QUESTION TIME

Usually on a Saturday morning as I passed the bus stop on my way to work, there was a bustling queue of people of all ages: young mums and toddlers heading for birthday parties at the soft play centre; teenagers homing in on the fast-food joints and cheap clothes shops; sporty types hitting the gym; pensioners meeting old friends at coffee shops.

This morning, however, not a soul was at the bus stop. *That's not very helpful for our campaign*, I thought crossly, before realising the reason for their absence. Anyone waiting for the bus wouldn't have been able to sit down because foliage and flowers covered the bus shelter's bench. This late in the year, many people's bedding plants had finished, so they'd fashioned wreaths from autumn leaves and evergreens instead. Here and there were bunches of shop-bought chrysanthemums in yellow and bronze. An acid-pink cyclamen seemed all the brighter for the black crepe ribbon tied around its terracotta pot.

When I turned in to Carol's shop, Maggie's surplus apples had been replaced by a black plastic bucket of bunched cut flowers. Carol caught me admiring them and blushed.

'Am I being callous, Sophie, to cash in on people's wish to lay flowers in the bus shelter in memory of Mrs Boggins? Ted kindly went down to the flower market this morning at crack of dawn and bought these for me to sell on.'

'No, not at all. I think you and Ted are being very thoughtful. It helps people to deal with a bereavement if they can do something constructive.'

I picked out a bunch of yellow chrysanthemums, and she handed me a small rectangular card with a black ribbon looped through it.

'For you to write your own tribute,' she explained.

I set the bouquet back in the bucket for a moment so as not to drip on the counter and picked up Carol's pen to write a message.

While I considered what to write, I glanced out of the shop window. The display looked impressive. I wished I'd bothered to read the tags for inspiration.

'I'm amazed at how many people have paid their respects already,' I said, which was code really for observing how unpopular Mrs Boggins was.

Carol leaned across the counter and lowered her voice. 'Most people round here heartily despised her, God rest her soul, but it still salivates their consciences to lay flowers.'

'Salves,' I said automatically. I prided myself on having learned to speak fluent Carol.

Was Carol hinting that Maggie Burton and Norman Arch weren't the only enemies Mrs Boggins had made in the village? And was anyone's enmity enough to make them murder her?

As I crossed the road from the village shop to the bus stop, Norma Cuts came stomping up the High Street, clutching an ivy wreath complete with scarlet berries. I tried to remember whether it was ivy berries or ivy leaves that were poisonous.

'So sad about poor Mrs Boggins,' I remarked as she arrived beside me.

Looping the wreath over her arm, Norma pulled a long nail from her jacket pocket and a large, heavy-headed hammer from her shopping bag.

She positioned the nail at the centre of the back wall of the bus shelter at about head height and gave it several hefty whacks. The strength in her spindly arms startled me.

'Yes, what a blamed nuisance,' she said tersely. 'She's completely distracted everyone from our campaign now. I can picture the headlines on *The Slate* next week: "Village grandmother dies on bus." Not a dicky bird about the need to save the bus service for the rest of us.'

She flung her wreath at the protruding nail as if trying her hand at the hoop-la on Village Show day. The wreath landed neatly on target. I wondered whether her aim was as accurate with a weapon.

* * *

Hector was unconvinced when I told him the theory I'd developed as I'd marched from the bus stop to the bookshop.

'Have you been reading too much Sherlock Holmes?' He laughed. 'I can't imagine where Norma Cuts would get a poison dart or a blowpipe.'

He had a point.

'Maybe. But don't you think it seems odd that no one noticed Janice dying on the bus? I mean, if it had been a heart attack, for example, people would have spotted her clutching her chest or her upper left arm or sweating and groaning.'

Hector turned his back to me to open the safe embedded in

the wall behind the trade counter and took out several bags of silver coins.

'Not necessarily. If she'd been asleep at the time of death, she might not have cried out. Or something else might have befallen her, like a stroke. She was quite old. Far more old people die of natural causes than from murder, if that's what you're driving at.'

'Not that old,' I protested, scooping up one bag of pound coins and another of fifty pence pieces as my tearoom float. 'People live to a lot older than her. Look at Joshua, next door to me.'

'But he leads a blameless life,' replied Hector. 'With no vices beyond his home-made wine.'

'And there's Billy.'

He closed the safe. 'Ah, now there you may have a point. Still, it's not really our business. We'll just wait and see what the post-mortem says. We must try not to lose any sleep over it in the meantime.'

As he fiddled with the dial to reset the safe combination, the shop door swung open to admit a family group with three children from the primary school.

'We'll have a busy day here today if more people are staying in the village rather than going into town. That'll help take our minds off it.'

As he turned round, a tall, broad-set gentleman with hair like a wire scouring pad entered the shop and approached the counter.

'Good morning, sir,' said the customer, with a formality uncommon in our usual clientele. He shot a sideways glance at me. 'Is there a Miss Sophie Sayers on the premises? I crave a moment of her time.'

He slipped his hand into his inside jacket pocket and pulled out a small flat leather wallet. For a moment I assumed it was a bus pass. Then he flipped it open and held it out for each of us to read.

I was grateful for his discretion in not announcing himself by name, so as not to alarm our customers.

'Hector, I think it would be a good idea if I took our visitor up to your flat, don't you?'

He fished in his jeans pocket for his flat key and passed it to me. As I led the visitor out of the shop and round the side to the front door to Hector's flat, I heard Hector say in a loud voice, 'Advance customers for our second-hand department are welcome, provided they make an appointment in advance.'

I'm not sure he fooled anyone.

* * *

'Please don't be alarmed, Miss Sayers, this is just a low-key enquiry, and no one is accusing or suspecting you of anything.'

'I should hope not!' I squealed, hoping Detective Inspector Easterbrook wouldn't interpret my shrill voice as a sign of a guilty conscience.

At least he was interrogating me in the comfort of Hector's flat rather than at the intimidating setting of a police station. Each of us sat in a high-backed dark green leather armchair, one on either side of the fireplace. Much more civilised than a stark grey room in a police station, drinking coffee out of plastic cups. I felt more like Dr Watson to the officer's Holmes, rather than suspect and detective. I half expected him to fish a cherry-wood pipe from his pocket and fill its deep bowl with his favourite tobacco, black shag. Instead, he took out a small electronic device and a stylus and jotted down a few notes.

'This is purely an information-gathering exercise while we

await the results of the post-mortem,' Detective Inspector East-erbrook continued, laying the tablet on his lap. 'We are just speaking informally to everyone on the bus the day Mrs Boggins died to gather witness statements. Don't worry, this is just routine. We just need to trace, interview, and eliminate. All part of the standard procedure.'

That was a relief.

Then he fished out a tiny audio recorder and clicked the 'on' button before setting it on the table between us.

The inspector steepled his fingers as he rested his elbows on the arms of the chair. They were exceptionally long, slender fingers. I bit back the urge to ask whether he played the violin. 'As you're probably aware, a post-mortem is required for any unexpected death in which the deceased had no known medical conditions and had not recently seen a healthcare professional. Most return a natural cause for death, whether a previously undetected fatal defect or an untreated condition. Most deaths will not have been preventable.'

'So, you think Mrs Boggins died of natural causes after all? I can't tell you how relieved that makes me feel.'

His fingers clenched and interlocked, his steeple collapsing into a pitched roof. 'You're relieved? How so?'

You fool, Sophie! I thought. *You're really messing this interview up. If you weren't a suspect already, you will be now.*

'Because – because I'd hate to think I'd been on a bus with a murderer.'

DI Easterbrook dropped his hands to his lap.

'Or rather, to know that if I'd been paying more attention to her, I might have spotted something amiss and saved her life.'

He picked up the stylus and stabbed at his tablet a few times. 'Are you medically trained, Miss Sayers?'

'Call me Sophie, please.' Since I'd stopped classroom teaching, only my mother had called me Miss Sayers, and only then when she was cross with me. His manner was making me feel guilty, but of what I was unsure. 'Only basic first aid, enough to get a certificate. But enough to know what to do if she'd been having a heart attack, or choking, or hypoglycaemic, or something.'

Choking? A chill ran through me.

Tucking into her picnic, Janice Boggins might easily have choked on a nut or a boiled sweet as the bus lurched over a pothole. There were loads of potholes between Wendlebury and Slate Green. But surely if she'd have choked, someone would have heard her?

'Not all causes of potentially fatal distress are as easy to detect and remedy. But we have an inkling of quite a different cause from which even a fully qualified doctor on board the bus would have been unable to prevent.'

I leaned forward, confidential, even though there was no one to overhear us. 'You mean poison?'

The inspector drew back, pressing his shoulders deep into the leather. 'Why would you think that?' He raised his eyebrows.

I decided for my own sake to come clean, my voice a throaty whisper. 'I know about the glue.'

He peered at me over the rim of his spectacles. 'You think Mrs Boggins had been sniffing glue? Unusual for someone of her generation.' He made a few more squiggles on his tablet. 'Surely someone would have noticed if she was doing it on board the bus.'

Was he bluffing to make me spill more details? If so, it was in very bad taste.

'No, not sniffing glue. But I wondered whether superglue might be poisonous if absorbed through the skin.'

His head on one side, the officer gazed at me for a moment through narrowed eyes before bursting out laughing.

'If you're an aspiring poisoner, Sophie, you're going about it all wrong. I don't for a moment assume you are the prankster who applied the superglue to the bus seat, but please be assured we have ruled that out as a method of – er – despatch.'

It seemed Tommy was going to get off lightly for his inadvertent prank. Her unrelated death had thrown her gluey skirt into perspective. I couldn't help but wonder whether her skirt was stuck to the seat even now. Perhaps they'd had to take her off the bus without her skirt. I guessed the bus must have been impounded for forensic tests.

As the inspector paused, looking down at his tablet, the laughter lines on his plump cheeks subsided, leaving only crinkles of worry at the corners of his eyes and from the outer edges of his nostrils to the corners of his mouth.

'But we have reason to suspect a certain substance played a part in her demise. We are therefore speaking to all her fellow passengers that day, on every journey, to investigate whether they saw her in any exchange of any kind with a fellow passenger. We are going to be speaking to all those who travelled on the 27 bus that day for all or part of Mrs Boggins' journey.'

Here was an opportunity to be helpful, making it clear that I was on the side of the police and not trying to obstruct the course of justice.

'I can tell you who shared my journey both ways,' I began.

The inspector waved a hand to interrupt.

'Don't worry, we know who was on the bus at all times, where they boarded, where they sat and where they disembarked. We already know, for example, how close you were sitting to Mrs Boggins and for how long you travelled together. The on-board video recorder captures a good likeness of everyone as they enter the bus and pay their fare or show their bus pass. For those who have either a season ticket or a senior citizen's card, we have a record of each of their trips recorded as they tap in and out on the driver's card reader.'

I couldn't resist looking for opportunities to trick the system. 'Supposing someone lends their bus pass to a friend?'

He peered at me over his glasses again. 'Fräulein Sayers, ve will ask ze questions.'

His German accent was straight out of *'Allo 'Allo!* When I failed to laugh, and shrank back slightly into my armchair, he gave an apologetic smile.

'Trust me, Sophie, the bus drivers are trained to prevent fraudulent use of bus passes. They check the photo against the bearer every time. Leif Oakham assured me it's a standard practice.'

I wanted to say, *Well, he would, wouldn't he?*, but I thought better of it.

'So, if you know who got on and off, and where and when, why did you come to see me? I'm not sure I can tell you anything you don't already know.'

'We don't know what we don't know, Sophie, so to get to the point, may I just ask: did you notice any event or incident or behaviour that might have compromised Mrs Boggins' safety, either man-made or otherwise, that our cameras might have missed? Unfortunately, although they are accurate enough to give the driver a broad impression of what his passengers are up to, the footage is grainier than your eyesight. So, was there anything unusual or remarkable about her behaviour on the two journeys you shared with her?'

I was silent for longer than I needed to formulate my answer, because I wanted the inspector to think I was racking my brains.

'No,' I said at last. 'I was sitting within sight of Mrs Boggins, and she kept herself to herself. She didn't even look at me but kept focused on her picnic. She was always nibbling at something, which I gather is perfectly normal for her. But' – I tried to be charitable – 'that day she was set for a long haul, putting in a nine-to-five shift on the bus in protest against the cuts, so she needed to keep her strength up.'

'Did she offer any of her snacks to anyone else? Did anyone offer to share their own food or drink with her?' The inspector was leaning forward again now, his elbows on his knees, his hands clasped loosely between his legs.

'No, nothing like that at all. The rest of us were abiding by the no-food-or-drink rule.'

He jabbed his tablet with his stylus some more, then finally closed the cover of his device, returned the stylus into its little loop at the edge of the case and slipped it back into his inside jacket pocket.

'Thank you, Sophie, you've been very helpful. In due course you will receive a hard copy of your statement for verification by signature. If, in the meantime, you remember anything else about the incident, please do not hesitate to contact me.'

He handed me his card.

Then he recited a standard instruction about making sure the police could contact me at any time. For a moment, I thought he was about to make the standard arrest statement: *I am arresting you on suspicion of the murder of Janice Boggins... You do not have to say anything, but...*

Then he remarked that his next stop would be Tommy's house.

As soon as I'd escorted the inspector down the stairs from the flat, out of the front door and into the street, I whipped my mobile out of my back pocket and texted a warning to Tommy. Thank goodness I had Tommy's mobile number. He'd insisted on my setting him up as a contact on my phone when he got his first mobile, even though I had no plans ever to call him. I was not about to encourage him to hide from the police. I just didn't want his mother to be terrified when a police officer turned up on her doorstep and jump to the false conclusion that either Tommy or his little sister Sina might be in trouble with the law – or, indeed, that she might be herself.

17

THE OLD BAG

Returning to the shop, I waited for a lull in trade before telling Hector the gist of my conversation with the police officer.

'So, Bob was right,' he said, frowning. 'I wonder what there was about the state of her body to make them suspect foul play. Otherwise, they wouldn't be sending police officers out to take witness statements.'

'Witness?' I gulped. 'Goodness, I hadn't thought of myself as an official witness. Do you think I'll have to give evidence in court?'

Hector raised his eyebrows. 'Could be worse. They could have you down as a perpetrator.'

'Oh, thanks a lot, Hector. That's small comfort.'

'Sorry, sweetheart. Now, who else did you say got on the bus with you that morning?'

'Just Norma – who would have seen Janice as a fellow campaigner – and Norman.'

'Wasn't Maggie Burton on the bus?'

'Nope. She was out and about. I saw her back retreating

down the High Street when I went to join the queue. She definitely wasn't on the bus.'

'Okay, that's her off the hook for all her talk of Janice poisoning her cat. Even if she had been tempted to stage a tit-for-tat assault on Janice, she wasn't on the bus, so couldn't have been Janice's attacker. How about Norman? Did he converse with her at all? I'd expect some argy-bargy if those two were in close quarters for any length of time.'

'No, he just dashed past her – and me – didn't even stop to put his bag in the luggage rack, although it looked quite hefty. He kept bumping it against the edges of the seats as he passed down the bus, and then looking annoyed at it, as if he was cross with it for drawing attention to him when he was trying to sidle past us unnoticed.'

Hector stroked his chin in thought. 'What sort of bag? A shopping bag? A sports bag?'

I frowned. 'Now that I think of it, it was an old-fashioned canvas zip-up holdall. I remember fearing for its seams, as it was packed fit to bust.'

'And did Norman return on your bus? Have you seen him since?'

I shook my head. 'Not that I'd usually cross paths with him. I'm even less likely to now, after our run-in over the shelves. He'll probably go out of his way to avoid me until the embarrassment fades.'

At that moment, the shop door creaked open. I glanced at my watch. It was the eleven o'clock Billy, on the dot as usual.

'Morning, Bill,' said Hector, looking more than usually pleased to see him. 'Tell me, were you at The Bluebird last night at all?'

Billy frowned and tapped his cheek with a forefinger, then

he stuffed his hands abruptly in his jacket pockets. 'Course I was, boy. Ain't I always on a Friday night? Darts night.'

Hector's face brightened. 'Norman Arch plays darts, doesn't he?'

'Yes, but not on my team, praise be, because his aim is rubbish. I often play against him. But not last night I didn't. Because he weren't there to play. Done a bunk, rumour has it. Upped and offed from his mum's on Friday taking all his worldly goods with him.'

'What?' I dropped the keys to Hector's flat on the floor and bent to pick them up again.

'Well, that's my theory, anyway,' said Billy. 'You upset him over those shelves, boy.'

'If those were all his worldly goods in that old bag he was carrying on the bus, he didn't have many of them.'

Billy shrugged and trudged towards his favourite table. 'How am I to know? That's just what folks is saying. For all I know, it could have been full of banknotes. He could have been stashing his wages under the floorboards for years, and just put them all in his bag for the journey to wherever he's running away to. Probably planning to buy everything he needs new when he gets there. Come to think of it, he had to ask Carol to change a tenner for coins before he joined the bus queue. I'm just guessing. Don't listen to an old man if you don't want to.'

I laid Hector's flat key on his desk and strolled over to rustle up Billy's cappuccino. Although making inconsequential small talk with him as I did so, I was thinking all the while that he could be onto something. If that bag was full of money, it would be a good disguise – the holdall looked cheap and tatty, and no one would ever believe it contained anything of value. But where might he get that much cash? And what did that have to do – if anything – with Janice's sudden death?

As I set Billy's cappuccino in front of him, he startled me by appearing to have developed the power of clairvoyance.

'I wouldn't go blaming old Norman for what happened to Janice Boggins, though,' he said out of the blue. 'No, I'd wager it's Maggie Burton, seeking revenge for poisoning one of her cats. An eye for an eye, like the good book says.'

'The good book might say that, but a British court of law doesn't. Besides, I wouldn't consider the life of Janice Boggins as equivalent to Maggie's cat. It's a lot longer, for a start.'

Billy put his hands over his ears in mock horror. 'Don't you let your little cat Blossom hear you talk like that. Anyway, I'm not justifying Maggie Burton poisoning Janice. I'm just reminding you that not so long ago, she said she'd like to do it. You're not the only one round here who can play the sleuth, Sophie Sayers.'

He was right. Maggie Burton's words echoed in my ears: *'I'd like to give her a taste of her own medicine.'* But how could she have administered poison to Janice if she wasn't on the bus?

Too many theories were buzzing in my head all afternoon. That included taking into account the many other passengers who had boarded the bus at other stops along the way, before and after Wendlebury. It might have been someone from a neighbouring village who had decided to murder Janice Boggins. But how, and who?

I was more than ready to shut up shop at closing time and retreat to Hector's flat to consider the facts away from the hubbub of our customers. While Hector set to work cooking us a delicious fish pie, I did the next best thing to playing Sherlock Holmes' violin to help me think. I sat down at the piano, put my fingers on the keys and waited for Beethoven to work his magic on my subconscious.

18

THE NEW RING

Just as Hector had donned the oven gloves to take the fish pie out of the oven, a rapid rat-a-tat-tat sounded at the flat's front door. I stopped playing the piano mid-tune, resting my hands in my lap as I gave Hector a quizzical look, and he just shrugged.

'I'm not expecting anyone,' he replied, replacing the oven gloves over the rail of the cooker and turning the control knob to reduce the temperature.

'Let's hope it's not that police officer back again,' I remarked. 'I'm hungry.'

Hector trotted down the stairs to the front door, and I strained my ears for clues as to the caller. A loud but unmistakeably feminine sigh of relief mixed with distress tipped me off straight away: to my surprise, it was Carol. I'd never known her to call on either of us at home before. Although I considered her a close friend, we conducted our relationship entirely in public places, such as her shop. Seeing her follow Hector up the stairs now and sit in one of his fireside chairs felt oddly intrusive. As Hector fetched a bottle of chilled white wine from the fridge and three wine glasses, clutching all three stems in one hand like a fragile bouquet, I wondered what occasioned her unprecedented home visit.

Her demeanour suggested it wasn't just a social call. Dried tears streaked her face, and it took her a minute to get her breath back.

'Is everything all right, Carol?' I asked as Hector poured the first glass of wine for her. 'It's lovely to see you, of course, but I'm assuming something has happened for you to call round at this time on a Saturday.'

She sniffed, presumably to clear her airways, but she can't have failed to notice the delicious aroma of our fish pie.

'Have you eaten yet this evening, Carol?' asked Hector. 'If not, you're welcome to stay and have supper with us. There's plenty to go round.'

Carol put her hands on the arms of the chair to launch herself to her feet. 'Oh, I'm sorry, Hector, I've come at a bad time for you. It's just that Ted's gone back to his house for the evening, and I had to see you without his knowledge. Please don't let me spoil your romantic *dîner à deux*.'

She pronounced the last word as 'ducks'.

Hector set the wine bottle on the coffee table and laid his hand gently on her shoulder. 'Don't be silly. You won't spoil our evening at all. We'd love you to have supper with us, wouldn't we, Sophie?'

'Do stay, Carol,' I added. 'I can see you've got something you need to talk to us about. And Hector's fish pie is delicious.'

Carol sniffed the air again, this time in appreciation. 'Well, if you're sure...'

Hector immediately went to the cutlery drawer to set a third place at the breakfast bar. He doesn't have space for a dining table in his flat, giving priority to his large, comfy easy chairs and many, many bookshelves. His entire living room is essen-

tially a reading nook which just happens to include a kitchenette and breakfast bar. It occurred to me that Carol might find
it easier to talk to us if we all sat alongside each other at the
breakfast bar, rather than facing us across the coffee table, like a
suspect being interrogated by police. One always confides in
another more readily when travelling side-by-side in a car than
when face-to-face.

Noting she wasn't wearing her engagement ring, I feared
she'd had a row with Ted. My heart sank. As I'd been instru-
mental in getting them together, it was a blow to me as well as to
Carol if it hadn't worked out. But I felt selfish for even thinking
of my pride. Ted was Carol's world.

Carol and I made small talk about the weather until Hector
was ready to serve up steaming plates of fish pie, juicy chunks of
pink, white and yellow basking in a creamy sauce beneath
mashed potato as light as a cloud. Carol savoured the first
mouthful before telling us the reason for her visit.

'It's my engagement ring.'

Hector and I both glanced involuntarily at where it should
have been on her left hand.

'I've lost it,' she added.

I laid down my knife and fork and breathed a sigh of relief.
'Oh, thank goodness! I thought you were going to tell us you and
Ted had split up.'

A fleeting smile passed across her face.

'Oh no, Sophie, nothing like that. Except...' Her face crumpled as she stared at her plate. 'Except when he finds out I've
been so careless with something so valuable, he may call it off in
disgust.'

I laid a hand on her arm to comfort her. 'I'm sure he'd never
do that. Your Ted's a keeper, and he thinks you are too. Don't
worry, I expect it'll turn up. You've probably just put it down

somewhere and forgotten it. Do you take it off to do the washing up? Have you checked by your kitchen sink? I'm forever losing earrings, but they generally turn up again in the flat or the shop or my cottage unless it's when I'm out and about. And you don't go out as much as I do, do you, Carol?'

She shook her head. 'No, but I know where I was when I lost it.'

'Then surely it's not lost?' said Hector, spearing a prawn.

He didn't seem to understand how precious Carol's long-awaited engagement ring might be for its significance rather than its material value.

Carol took a large swig of wine before continuing. 'But that's exactly it. It shouldn't have been able to get lost. I was in the shop, and I set it down on the counter for Janice Boggins to try on – all my friends have been wanting to try it on, as it's so fancy – and then Norman Arch tried to queue-jump to get change for the bus, and I had to check his fifty-pound note with my special pen for counterparts—'

'Counterfeits,' I translated for Hector.

'Then when I put his change on the counter, half the coins rolled onto the floor by my feet, and I had to crawl about on my hands and knees to pick them all up again. Don't you remember, Sophie?'

She turned to me for verification, and I gave an encouraging nod. 'Yes, I was starting to get worried that Norman's interruption was going to make us all miss the bus.'

'Then, just as I was getting up from the floor, a stranger came in asking for directions to Maggie Burton's house, saying he was lost. It was only when I'd sorted him out, and made the two take-away coffees he wanted, and the bus was just pulling away from the bus stop, that I realised my left hand felt funny, and I looked down and there the ring wasn't.'

'You think Norman waltzed off with it?' asked Hector. I knew he was still smarting from his row with Norman over the shelves, but that was no reason to brand him a thief.

'Innocent until proven guilty,' I reproved him.

'I don't know what to think,' replied Carol. 'I suppose he could have swept it up along with the coins I'd just given him and slipped it into his trouser pocket while I was under the counter.'

'Surely Janice Boggins would have stopped him from doing that?'

I didn't much like Janice, but I couldn't picture her as Norman Arch's partner-in-crime.

'Hang on, I thought Janice was trying the ring on,' said Hector.

'I doubt he'd have wrestled it off her hand,' I remarked.

Carol laid down her knife and fork, rested her elbows on the breakfast bar and put her head in her hands. 'I don't know.' Her voice was cracking. 'I just don't know anything any more. I'm just a foolish old woman. I don't know what Ted sees in me. I don't deserve him and his beautiful ring.'

I slipped my arm around her quaking shoulders. 'Now come off it, Carol. For a start, you're not the least bit old, and anyone with half a brain can see Ted adores you. Besides, the ring can't have vanished into thin air. Goodness knows, the gemstone was big enough to be unmissable. Are you sure it didn't fall on the floor along with Norman's loose change? If it fell at the same time as a load of coins, you wouldn't have heard it fall. It's probably just rolled under the counter and is sitting there waiting for you to find it.'

'What a treasure that would be for a Borrower to find,' mused Hector.

I frowned at him. 'What are you on about?'

He was not exactly being helpful.

Carol lifted her face and gave a watery smile. 'Oh, you know, Sophie, those tiny people in Mary Norton's books for children. They live behind the wainscoting and sneak people's darning needles and other little things they might find useful when we're not looking. I know I can never find a darning needle when I want one.'

I didn't know anyone still did darning.

I waved aside his diversion. 'Anyway, I suggest you take a long knitting needle and run it under the counter and into every nook and cranny about the floor. Or might it have fallen into those big baskets of apples beside the counter? Have you tipped them all out to check?' An alarming thought struck me. 'Goodness, you haven't put them onto your compost heaps, have you? I wouldn't blame you if you had. They were starting to go over when I was last in the shop.'

Carol was staring into the distance.

'I knew I should never have persuaded Mum to let Norman off when she caught him pinching KitKats,' she said. Carol's parents, who had run the shop before she had, died many years before. 'He was only little then, of course, when Mum was still alive. But he was always a bit light-fingered, as some kids are, but she thought a second chance and forgiveness would do more good than telling his mum, who would have just whacked him. He was a frail, skinny boy at that stage, so he might not have got enough to eat at home. You wouldn't think it to look at him now, nor his brother, neither.'

'If Norman hadn't done his disappearing act, the sensible thing would have been for you just to ask him if he'd seen the ring,' said Hector. 'If he had stolen it, you would have given him the opportunity to own up and return it and save himself from getting into trouble. You might even have allowed him to pretend he scooped it up by accident along with his change. That way you'd have given him a second chance, same as your mum would have done. And if he pretended to know nothing about it, you'd have had reasonable grounds to report your suspicions to the police for them to investigate.'

The simplicity of this solution was genius. I was glad for the reminder of Hector's essential kindness, after Norman had brought out his less generous side.

Carol gazed into her glass for a moment. 'You know, I'd quite geared myself up to report him to the police when they came to ask me for any information I might have about Janice's death. I was sure they would want to talk to me, given that I've got such a good view of the bus stop, and that I was there all day when Janice was going back and forth on the bus. But they haven't. But when they passed me by, I took that as a sign that I shouldn't tell them about my missing ring. Everything happens for a reason, my mum always used to say.'

Hector topped up our wine glasses. 'You don't need to correlate the two incidents – Janice's death and the loss of your ring. I very much doubt they're related. Besides, the police officer who was gathering evidence for Janice's murder will only be interested in anything related to her death.'

'God rest her soul,' said Carol, raising her glass.

'The police won't have time to look for lost property,' Hector continued.

'No matter how valuable,' I added, anxious not to shatter Carol's illusion that the ring was a real diamond. 'If you like, you could report it as a separate crime, which you'll need to do to get a crime reference number, if that makes you feel better.'

Hector gave me a warning glance, reminding me that the truth about the ring's low value would have to come out if she made an insurance claim.

Carol held the cool bowl of her wine glass against her flushed cheek. 'Perhaps you're right, Hector, although I don't know whether I've left it too late now. He might have pawned it or sold it by now. It could be miles away. As it seems Norman Arch is now, too.'

* * *

'I don't want to seem callous,' said Hector, once Carol had gone home, and we were sitting comfortably in the fireside chairs enjoying an after-dinner coffee. 'But isn't this a lot of fuss about not very much? I mean, the ring's only cubic zirconia. It's probably only worth about fifty quid.'

I lifted a bare foot to prod his knee reprovingly. 'The money's not the issue. I'm more worried about Carol having to tell Ted she's lost her valuable diamond ring, only for him to tell her it was a cheap imitation. Still, their relationship is probably strong enough to withstand it.'

'If Norman has stolen it for his own gain, I'd like to see his face when he takes it to a dealer only to be told it's cheap costume jewellery.' Hector chuckled.

'Well, before Carol does anything else, she needs to go home and turn the shop upside down looking for it before she accuses anybody to their face. She has no real evidence that Norman stole it. It might just as easily have been Janice, or even the stranger who came in asking for directions to Maggie Burton's house.'

'Or even you,' said Hector, diluting the sting of his accusation with a wink. 'After all, you were in the shop when all this was going on.'

My mouth fell open in surprise. I'd just cast myself in the

role of omniscient observer. It had never occurred to me that someone might consider me a suspect.

His eyes twinkling in mischief, Hector turned sideways on his bar stool, leaned forward and put his hands on my knees. 'Actually, perhaps her visit just now was a subtle ploy to give you the chance to confess and return the ring.'

I slapped his hand. 'Yes, you've rumbled me. Any minute now I'm going to produce the ring from my pocket and propose.'

Even joking about the prospect made my heart race. I was playing with fire.

Hector stayed my hand in mid-air and gave it an affectionate squeeze. 'I think we've got enough trouble on our hands with one new engagement in the village, don't you?'

I grinned. 'Absolutely. But going back to Norman, don't you find it suspicious that he's the only passenger on the bus that hasn't returned to the village since Janice was found dead? Surely, he must be prime suspect for her murder, even if not for stealing Carol's ring.'

We'd both stopped smiling now.

'Although how he, or anyone else, killed her will only become apparent when we hear the results of the post-mortem.'

19

THE SILENT CAR

Next morning, looking forward to spending the day with Hector, I popped back to my cottage after breakfast to feed Blossom and open a few windows to let in some fresh air. Although there was a definite autumnal nip in the air, the sun was still strong enough to warm your skin when the wind dropped.

'What would you think of having Hector living here?' I asked Blossom as I squeezed meaty chunks in jelly from a sachet into her food dish.

She gave a single mew, arched her back and rubbed her cheek against my ankle before the whiff of the cat food diverted her attention. Hector was more of a dog person than a cat person, and Blossom had yet to win him over, but at least he wasn't allergic.

On my way back up the high street to Hector's, on a whim, I called in at the village shop to buy a Sunday newspaper. Sharing the Sunday paper with Hector, swapping the various supplements as we finished with them and reading interesting snippets aloud to each other seemed a cosy, grown-up way to start a lazy

Sunday, before we set to work on transforming his flat into the new second-hand department.

To my relief, Carol was looking a little brighter and was free of tearstains. After choosing my newspaper, I dithered in front of the confectionary shelves, waiting for the only other customer to leave the shop so that I could talk to Carol in confidence about her missing ring. Carol seemed to have the same idea. As soon as the cyclist she was serving had departed, she came out from behind the counter and bustled up beside me. When she began to speak in a low voice, I guessed Ted was on the premises, probably in the stockroom at the back. I glanced at her left hand, hoping to see her ring there, but her finger was still bare.

'Sophie! I need to speak to you!' she said, unnecessarily. 'I've spent all night thinking about Friday morning, trying to re-enact exactly what happened, to trace my missing you-know-what, and I've realised there is a missing piece of the hacksaw.'

Jigsaw.

I nodded to encourage her to continue.

'You see, there was someone else at the bus stop who spoke to Janice Boggins before you and Norman and Norma Cuts got there. I was thinking if Janice had stolen the you-know-what, that could have been her – what do they call it on cop shows on the telly? Her brick wall?'

I thought for a moment. 'Her fence? Someone who would handle the stolen goods for her?'

I put back on the shelf two bars of chocolate I'd been trying to choose between. This new revelation was far more interesting.

'But how would she have known she'd have the chance to steal your ring at that time, to arrange in advance for her accomplice to swing by?'

'Oh, that's easy. She just had to ask me for her turn to try on my ring. I would hardly have refused after letting so many others try it for size. And no one would have been surprised to see Janice or anyone else turn up at the bus stop after all the fighting talk at the parish council meeting.'

'So, who was her accomplice? Anyone you recognised? Someone from the village?'

'Actually, I'm not sure,' replied Carol, furrowing her brow in thought. 'I didn't recognise the big black car they were in, so I don't think so. Besides, not many local cars stop at the bus stop, because they know you're meant to keep the road beside it clear for buses, so if I'm at the till, by the window, I usually notice them because they're unusual. This car was unusual all right because it was so silent. I didn't hear it pull up. I only spotted it once it had stopped. It made me jump to see it appear there unannounced, as if it had just beamed down from outer space, like Captain Cook in *Star Trek*.'

Kirk.

'Did you see who was driving it?'

She considered for a moment. 'A man in a hat. You know, a peaked cap like a chauffeur.'

'Like the one that was driving Leif Oakham away from the emergency parish council meeting the other night? I noticed Oakham got into the back seat rather than the driving seat, so he must have had a chauffeur.'

Carol brightened. 'Yes, it was a car like that. One of those newfangled Tefal cars that runs off the electric. Amazing what they can do these days, although I'm not sure I'd want to drive about in one made of the same stuff as frying pans.'

'You mean Tesla, not Tefal. And yes, it is relatively silent. You probably wouldn't hear a low whir like that through the plate-glass shop window. Much quieter than, say, the bus pulling up at the bus stop.'

Carol's cheeks were getting pinker.

'Yes, you're right. And I'd kept the shop door shut, rather than propped open, as it was a chilly morning.'

'If it was Leif Oakham, he was hardly likely to be there to act as a fence for your stolen ring. I've heard he's loaded. Highwayman is just one of his many enterprises.'

'Shh!' She put her finger to her lips and nodded towards the stockroom. 'I still haven't told Ted I've lost it.'

'Sorry.' I lowered my voice. 'But in that case, what was Leif Oakham doing talking to Janice?'

Carol shrugged. 'Maybe he just wanted to see for himself how many passengers were using the bus, or to regain some goodwill for his company, after upsetting everyone at the parish council meeting. If so, it's a shame he spoke only to Janice. She's not the best ambassador for the village.'

'Did you see him speak to anyone else?'

Carol considered for a moment. 'No, he didn't stop long. He was gone by the time Norman got out there, and Norma too, of course. And now that I think about it, I didn't actually see Mr Oakham, just his car and his chauffeur. The car was between us, you see, and I only saw the back of his head when he got out of the car, as the rest of him was hidden by the car in between us. So I couldn't swear it was him. I only saw his front at that meeting. We all did.'

'No, but I know who might have done,' I put in. 'Maggie Burton. She was walking away from the bus stop as I crossed the road from the village shop to join the queue. He might even have spoken to her before he spoke to Janice. I'll see if I can track down Maggie and ask her.'

'Please don't tell her about the you-know-what, though,' Carol implored in a whisper. 'Or else it'll be all over the village.'

'Don't worry, I won't. By the way, I don't suppose you

remember the number on the licence plate of the Tesla? That way we can confirm whether it was Leif Oakham's or not.'

It was a long shot, but it was worth an ask.

'No, I couldn't because it was sideways on to me, right opposite the shop. I couldn't see the front or back. Besides, I must have had my reading glasses on rather than my distance ones, because when it pulled away, the number was just a blur. I probably wouldn't have remembered it anyway, as at that time I had no reason to do so. Besides, I was busy looking for my ring. Sorry, Sophie.'

I returned my attention to the chocolate shelf, picked up a bar of Galaxy and together we headed for the front of the shop so that I could pay for my purchases – cash this time, as it wasn't for Hector's House.

'Not to worry. Perhaps someone else will have spotted the Tesla in the village that morning. Chances are, someone will have recognised Leif Oakham in it as there were so many of us who saw him in the flesh at the parish council meeting.'

If this had happened in London, or even Slate Green, chances are someone would have captured the strange car on a security camera, and it would have been child's play to trace its occupants, whether Leif Oakham or someone entirely different.

As I headed back up to Hector's House, for the first time I regretted the absence of CCTV cameras in Wendlebury Barrow.

20

PLANTING OUT

'Why don't you just call Leif Oakham and ask if it was him?' said Hector, as I broke the bar of Galaxy in two and gave him the bigger piece.

'How very sensible,' I replied, biting off a square of chocolate. 'Why didn't I think of that? After all, he could have been one of the last people to speak to Janice Boggins before she died. I'll phone his secretary tomorrow morning on some pretext. For example, I could say he'd dropped something personal at the bus stop and we wanted to check it was his before returning it.'

Hector raised his eyebrows. 'Something like a diamond ring?'

'Ha! I don't think so. I'll think of something. A receipt or a ticket, perhaps. It was a breezy morning, so something papery could easily have wafted out of the car door as he opened it. An important-looking receipt, for example.'

I went to look out of the front window of the flat to assess the weather now.

'It's quite still out there now. I almost took my jacket off as I was so warm walking back from the village shop earlier. Shall we take advantage of the calm to replant the troughs outside the bookshop before we get stuck into putting up the new bookshelves?'

Hector opened a lower kitchen cupboard and extracted a small wooden trug bearing an immaculate stainless steel hand fork and trowel. He set a high bar for order and tidiness. If he was going to move into my cottage, I'd need to give my garden shed a spring clean first and rub the rust off my tools.

He slipped them into the cardboard box of chrysanthemum plants I'd bought on my bus trip to Slate Green, and we headed down the stairs and onto the street.

Working as a team, we uprooted the straggly remnants of summer bedding plants. Hector shook off the excess soil from their roots and chucked them in the green bin while I fished out a few remaining bits of root and the odd weed. As I started to bed in the new plants, Hector went to fetch a jug of water from the tearoom. He'd only just gone when Tommy and Sina on their bikes screeched to a halt on the pavement beside me, so close that they made my shirt flutter.

'I'd have done that for you if you'd asked,' said Tommy, bypassing any kind of greeting. 'I'm good at weeding. Billy said so.'

'We both could have done it,' said Sina. She was always keen to muscle in on any opportunity to earn a reward. Our usual currency was free drinks and snacks from the tearoom.

'Too late, I'm just about done now,' I said, halfway through the second trough. 'But thanks for offering.'

I didn't like to discourage their enthusiasm. Entrepreneurial skills were useful in a village with virtually no local jobs.

'Never mind,' said Tommy in a tone that suggested their late arrival was my loss more than theirs. 'So, you want to hear my theory?'

I tamped down the soil around the base of the last chrysanthemum, then stood up, arching my back to stretch it after crouching over the troughs.

'What theory is that, Tommy?' I was anticipating some batty notion about the mystical power of chrysanthemums or cutting earthworms in half to make two new living creatures.

'Cyanide...' He paused for effect.

'What, as a weedkiller?' My mind was still on gardening.

'As an old lady killer,' he replied. 'I reckon that's what killed old Bogroll.'

'He thought it was his superglue that killed her at first,' put in Sina. 'But I told him it's not like she ate it. Anyway, my mum said superglue couldn't possibly have got through Mrs Boggins' thick knickers. You can see Mrs Boggins' washing hanging on the line from our upstairs windows.'

With a pang, I realised that dubious joy would never happen again.

'Whatever makes you think she was poisoned with cyanide, Tommy?'

'Well, it's obvious, isn't it? Anyone could make cyanide if they put their mind to it.'

'Really?' I hoped he hadn't been trying his hand at it in his bedroom.

'Yes, didn't you know there's cyanide in apple pips? That's why you should never eat apple cores.'

'There's this boy at school who eats apple cores, but I don't like him much, so I haven't told him,' added Sina.

I bit my lip. 'Yes, but it's present in such a tiny quantity that eating the occasional apple core wouldn't be enough to harm anyone. They'd need to eat them by the barrelful.'

'Well, Maggie Burton is giving away apples by the barrelful,' replied Tommy. 'You must have seen all those apples in the shop.'

'Yes, but I haven't seen Mrs Boggins eating them, cores and all.'

I thought it better not to tell him I'd seen her eating an apple on the bus.

'No, but Mrs Boggins might have extracted all the pips and baked them into flapjacks or squished them into a smoothie or something.'

'My mum makes cakes that are all seedy like that,' said Sina. 'She thinks they're healthy. Then she wonders why we won't eat them.'

I was unnerved by how far Tommy had thought this through.

'Or it could have been cherry stones,' he added. 'There's cyanide in cherry stones too.'

That was alarming news. I'd accidentally swallowed a cherry stone the previous week. I cleared my throat, as if subconsciously trying to regurgitate it. I tried to remain calm. You couldn't fit much of anything in a cherry stone, including cyanide.

'Tommy, have you got your phone on you?'

'Of course.' He whisked it out of his back pocket with the flourish of a conjurer producing a rabbit from a hat. He hadn't had it for long, and it was still a novelty.

'Would you mind just googling how many apple cores and cherry stones make a fatal dose?'

While he tapped in a search, I scooped up the soil that had fallen outside of the troughs with my trowel and sprinkled it around the base of the chrysanthemums.

'Fourteen cherry stones,' Tommy announced. 'Or around

thirty apple cores.' He looked up from his phone. 'Or I guess you could have a bit of each. Mix and match.'

Sina put her hands on her hips.

'I'd rather eat fourteen cherry stones than thirty apple cores,' she said. 'It would take ages to eat thirty apple cores, and just think of all those awful hard bits like toenail clippings that would get stuck in your teeth.'

Hector reappeared from the shop, water jug in hand. He'd taken so long I suspected him of trying to avoid Tommy and Sina, but I was glad if he'd thought better of it. Both children were very fond of him. They'd probably remember him for the rest of their lives as the funny old bookseller from their child-hood, even though he was only thirty-one now.

I brought him up to speed with our conversation. 'Tommy and Sina are just telling me how many apple cores and cherry stones it takes to kill a person.'

'What, you mean if they fall on their head?' replied Hector cheerfully. 'Several tons, I should think.'

Sina frowned. 'No, silly, if you swallow them. It's fourteen cherry stones, thirty apple cores.'

She made it sound like a recipe or a medical prescription.

Hector shrugged. 'I can't imagine anyone managing to eat thirty apple cores in one go.'

'That's what I said,' said Sina, looking at Tommy.

'Although it would be easy enough to swallow fourteen cherry stones, if you really wanted to,' Hector continued, 'You'd need the digestive system of an ox to process them and extract the cyanide through the hard shell. Or a stomach like a grindstone to break them apart. I'd expect them to go straight through you undigested.'

Sina's face was the picture of disgust.

'Why?' asked Hector. 'I hope you're not planning on trying it out? And I hope it's not some silly dare doing the rounds on social media. I wouldn't go near it if I were you. There are less risky ways to get your five-a-day.'

'Yes, too much fruit is bad for you.' Sina waved an admonishing finger at him. 'Look what happened to Mrs Boggins. She loved fruit and now she's stone dead. Cherry-stone dead.'

Hector's face fell. 'Sorry, I wouldn't have been so frivolous if I'd known you were talking about poor Mrs Boggins.'

Tommy stuffed his phone into the back pocket of his jeans.

'Well, that's my theory, anyway,' he said, wiping his hands together dismissively. 'Sina's got her own, haven't you, Sina?'

Sina took a couple of steps towards me and lowered her voice.

'If you ask me, it was chewing gum that did it. Haven't you heard? If you swallow chewing gum, it wraps itself around your heart, and you die.' With a forefinger, she drew a squiggly circle on her chest.

Hector passed a hand over his mouth to smooth away his smile. 'Well, these are both interesting theories, but I think we'd better let the doctors decide.'

Sina's eyebrows shot up in surprise. 'Have they taken her to the doctors? I'd have thought it was too late for that. Or have they brought her back to life?'

Tommy rolled his eyes at his little sister's foolishness. 'Not the sort of doctor we go to when we're poorly. Bogroll will be sent to a special doctor for dead people, won't she, Sophie? For a post-partum?'

'Post-mortem,' corrected Hector, biting his lower lip hard.

'By a forensic pathologist,' I added.

Tommy shrugged. 'Whatever.'

When Hector turned his back on the children to start

watering in the chrysanthemums, his shoulders were shaking with silent laughter.

'Actually, we don't know yet what she died of,' I pointed out. 'Let's not jump the gun.'

Tommy shook his head. 'Oh, I don't think she was shot, Sophie. Even with a silencer, everyone on the bus would have seen the blood. By the way, I don't suppose you've got any apples in the tearoom, have you?' Tommy looked hopefully through the open shop door. 'I could just fancy an apple.'

I closed the door quickly. 'Sorry, Tommy, I haven't, and the tearoom's closed. It's Sunday, remember?'

'Okay, we'll be off, then. Come on, Sina.'

Tommy sat back on the saddle of his bike, and with a jangle of bicycle bells, the pair of them sped off to the play park.

I stared after them for a moment.

Hector slipped his arm around my shoulders.

'Still hankering after two wheels instead of four? Just remember, as far as the business is concerned, two wheels bad, four wheels good. So, do you fancy going out for another driving lesson this afternoon? I suppose we should give it another go. We shouldn't let the other night put us off. Second time lucky, ha-ha.'

I reached up for his hand resting on my shoulder and gave it a little squeeze.

'Actually, Hector, I was wondering whether it might make more sense if I invested in one of those intensive driving courses, to get it over with quickly? The sort where they guarantee you'll pass your test in a week? The sooner I've got my licence, the sooner I can really pull my weight, both in the business and offering people lifts once the bus has stopped running.'

How much longer was he going to let me waffle on before agreeing? I was really giving it my all.

'I can afford it,' I added, wondering whether he'd been feeling obliged to teach me himself to save me the cost of driving school lessons. 'My dad told me last week that the next tranche of royalties from Auntie May's books is due this week.'

Auntie May generously made me her copyright heir, which means I will receive royalties on her books for the first seventy years after her death. I hope her books will never go out of print.

'Well, if you put it like that, it would be churlish of me to disagree.' I could hear the relief in his voice. 'Let's go inside now and search online for courses.'

Yes, I thought, *before I lose my nerve.*

21

TWO WHEELS GOOD

In my excitement at finding myself booked onto a driving course starting the very next day, I'd almost forgotten my quest to discover whether it had been Leif Oakham's electric car at the bus stop on the Friday morning. Besides, there was nothing I could do about it on a Sunday. There was no point trying to phone his office until Monday, as no one would be there to answer the phone.

As I was walking back to my cottage late afternoon, I spotted Kate gliding along the high street towards me on her electric bike. She gave me a cheerful wave and pulled up at the kerb road to speak to me. I was excited to tell her my news. She planted her feet on the ground, steadying the bike between her knees while she adjusted the chinstrap on her helmet.

'Hi, Kate! Guess what? I'm starting an intensive driving course tomorrow. By the end of Thursday, I should have my licence – guaranteed, or my money back!'

'Really? Interesting business model. Best of luck to you. And will you run your own car when you pass, or use Hector's?'

'I hadn't thought that far ahead, but I suppose I should buy my own. At least then when the bus service is no more, I can give people lifts.'

Then I remembered my mission. 'Speaking of buses, I don't suppose you know anyone around here who drives a big black electric saloon car?'

Kate was the most likely of anyone I knew to have friends with such expensive vehicles.

'Why, are you thinking of buying electric?'

That idea hadn't occurred to me either. Really, there were so many decisions to be made now I'd decided to learn to drive.

'No, this is to do with the awful business of Janice Boggins. Carol told me she saw someone with a chauffeur-driven black electric car speaking to Janice before she got on the bus on Friday morning. At least, the car was being driven by someone in a hat.'

Kate laughed. 'I wear a hat while I'm driving sometimes, especially if I've got the top down. But that doesn't make me a chauffeur.'

'It wasn't a convertible like yours. Janice appeared to be speaking to someone who got out of the back of the car. If anyone remembers the licence plate, it might be an important piece of evidence for the police. She might have told them she wasn't feeling well, or had palpitations, or something like that, which might suggest death by natural causes.'

Kate grinned. 'Oh Sophie, you old sleuth! Unfortunately, I don't think I know anyone with a black electric car of any kind. Although now you come to mention it, I noticed one on the high street on Friday morning, crawling along as if the driver was lost or looking for something, or maybe he was early for a meeting and was just taking his time. The car was going so slowly that I overtook it on my bike. The only things I usually overtake are horses.'

If we ever have traffic jams on the High Street, horses or tractors are usually the cause.

I glanced wistfully up at the nearest telegraph pole. 'What a shame we don't have CCTV around here. Not that I particularly want to live under constant surveillance, but technology has its uses.'

'Please don't wish CCTV on Wendlebury, Sophie. We'd far rather be left in peace. But anyway, that's where you're wrong.' Kate tapped her helmet. 'Because although there might not be any permanent CCTV cameras installed about the village – and long may that last – you see here your very own moving surveillance camera. Because, against my better judgement, I followed my dear husband's advice and bought one of these little compact cameras that clip onto a cycling helmet. Look!'

When she pointed to the little black box stuck to the top of her helmet, my heart skipped a beat.

'Kate, how long does it record for before it overwrites its memory?'

Kate tapped her upper lip with her forefinger. 'A couple of hours, I think.'

'And how much cycling have you done since your trip on Friday morning?'

'Oh, hardly any. I didn't take the bike out at all yesterday. So are you thinking—'

In my excitement, I couldn't help but interrupt. 'Yes, we'll be able to tell from your cycle helmet camera whether that was Leif Oakham speaking to Janice Boggins. And if it wasn't his car, we should be able to read the numberplate and trace the owner. Ooh, Kate, have you got a moment? Can we view your footage now?' I clasped my hands in front of my chest in a plea.

'Yes, that's fine by me, Sophie. I was just heading home now. Walk back with me, and I'll fire up the old PC, stick the camera's chip in it, and Bob's your uncle. Or Leif Oakham, or whoever else your man of mystery turns out to be.'

Kate insisted on wheeling her bike alongside me as we headed for her house, making small talk.

I was so eager to view the camera footage that if she'd cycled ahead, I'd have run after her.

'When I was a child, there were so few cars passing through the village that sometimes my friend Lucy and I used to sit on my front wall writing down the numbers of passing vehicles,' Kate said. 'I don't know what we thought we'd do with them. Still, it killed time on a quiet day in the school holidays.'

Even now, there wasn't so much passing traffic that it would be an impossible task.

We crunched up the long gravel drive to her house, and I had to wait for her to secure her expensive bike in a specially built low wooden shed, remove the battery, put it into the charging bracket and padlock the shed's doors. Finally, we entered her house through the open front door. Her husband, Mark, was somewhere within, and she called to him in greeting. We headed through the high-ceilinged hall, its Victorian tiled floor softened with antique Persian runners, and took the first door on the left to Kate's study, where I'd never set foot before.

The large square room provided a clear view of the drive and any approaching visitors, particularly from her vantage point at the broad double-pedestal oak desk situated in the tall bay window. It was covered with antique desk accessories, including two silver inkwells set into a crystal dish, a pencil pot made of some poor creature's foot, and a collection of family photos in ornate frames – including one of Hector with me. Among all this paraphernalia, the sleek black computer screen looked like a time-travelling visitor from the future.

Kate bent down to turn on the computer, its workings

concealed at the back of the deep footwell of the desk, before sitting in the swivel oak chair upholstered in tan leather so old it was cracking. She placed the helmet on her lap, pressed a button on the top, and the memory card in the camera popped out. Then she disappeared under the desk again to insert it into the computer's card reader.

'It'll take a minute or two to fire up,' she told me. 'Have a seat. Make yourself comfortable.'

Sinking into a soft, deep leather sofa against the wall, I surveyed Kate's wonderful collection of vintage and antiquarian books that lined all but one of the study walls. The other was reserved for businesslike folders and files relating to her many activities and committees. I was very glad she'd volunteered to man our second-hand department if we ever needed an extra pair of hands. The knowledge and taste that had enabled her to build up this collection would make her a real asset as we developed that line of our business.

'Here you go, Sophie,' she was saying, as I was halfway through counting the leather-bound volumes in a massive set of art encyclopaedias. I extricated myself from the deep sofa's embrace and went to peer over her shoulder at the screen.

'Look, here I am setting off from home on Friday morning. Or rather, here's what I was seeing as I set off. You can't see me, of course.'

It was rather fun to watch the village come towards the camera and disappear on either side. Several people waved or raised a hand or a walking stick in greeting as she cycled past them. Everybody in Wendlebury knew Kate. It must have been like being the late Queen, having everyone recognise her.

There was Tommy's mum, getting into her hatchback to head for work, and a young mum holding a toddler's hand as he stopped to examine a fallen leaf. Here was Maggie Burton, trudging towards her from the direction of the village shop, the bus stop behind her. Then the camera panned to the right, as the back of a big black car approached – or rather, as Kate on her bicycle approached the stationary electric car. She steered to the right to overtake it.

'Hang on, rewind!' she cried, fiddling with the mouse to pause the image, then play it backwards, frame by frame, until we had a clear view of the car's licence plate. 'Ooh, it's personalised!' she cooed. 'That shouldn't be hard to trace.'

'Actually, I think you can trace any car pretty easily these days,' I put in. 'Hector says the government has all the essential data on every vehicle in the country on their central computer – registration, keeper, tax, insurance. But hang on, that doesn't look like the personalised number plate Leif Oakham would have: GB 123. It's neither his initials nor relating to his company name.'

'Perhaps he's just very patriotic,' suggested Kate. 'Or mad about Brexit and wanted to show his political leaning.'

I grimaced. 'Let me write that down so I don't forget, and I'll do more research on my computer when I get home. I've got time before I pack for Dorset. I'm heading off very early tomorrow on the bus, then another bus from Slate Green to Bath, before catching the train from Bath to Casterbridge, in Dorset, where the driving school is.'

Kate turned round to look at me. 'Really? The driving course is residential?'

'It was the closest one I could find with a vacancy for this week, but I got a cut-price last-minute deal, and the money off will cover the cost of a budget hotel for the few days I'm down there. You never know, I might even drive myself home. They have a special arrangement with a local garage that offers discounts for new drivers.'

'Do you want me to fill in for you over at the shop?'

I shook my head. 'That's really kind of you, Kate, but I've spoken to Mrs Wetherley, and she was more than happy to stand in for me. Turns out she really enjoyed her stint covering the tea room while we were in Scotland, and she leaped at the opportunity for an action replay.'

I just hoped my bus journey wouldn't involve another passenger's demise.

22

TRACING THE NUMBER

Unfortunately, my attempt to trace the licence plate on my laptop that evening drew a blank. While it was relatively straightforward to find out unhelpful snippets of information like its MOT records, nowhere could I find the details of its owner. With a standard-issue licence plate, at least I'd have been able to tell from the first two letters its place of registration. Although that would inevitably have been a broad area, it would at least have been a starting point. Of course, its purchaser could have bought it far from where it had been first registered, and it might have changed ownership several times since then. However, I guessed someone wealthy enough to afford a Tesla might have bought it new from the showroom and kept it or had it custom made to suit their personal preferences of trim accessories, and so forth, so it seemed unlikely to have had a string of owners.

When I was on the verge of giving up, tiring of the adverts that kept popping up for sites selling personalised licence plates, I struck what I thought was gold: a government website with a downloadable PDF telling you seventeen ways to identify the registered keeper of a vehicle. We only needed one.

Sadly, it was fool's gold. Although there was an online form I could use to apply for information, none of the seventeen criteria listed applied to our situation. I didn't have evidence of the car being illegally parked on my property, for example. The civil servant processing my application would dismiss me as a nosy neighbour with too much time on their hands.

But when Hector arrived at seven o'clock for a farewell supper, he had rendered my search unnecessary.

'The thing is, Sophie, they've just arrested Norman Arch.'

'What? That was quick. How do you know?'

He looked slightly sheepish. 'I stopped at The Bluebird for a quick half on the way here, and Bob was standing at the bar waiting to be served before me. The family liaison officer had just been sent to tell Mr Boggins.'

'Where did they find Norman? Had he really fled the scene of the crime to start a new life on the proceeds of Carol's ring?'

'Oh, I'd almost forgotten about the ring. No, he'd gone to stay with his sister in Dorset for a few days. Hence his travelling bag on the bus. There was nothing dodgy about it – it just contained clothes, his toilet bag, razor, the usual short-break gear. His sister said she'd asked him to come and decorate her flat.'

I grimaced. 'She had a lucky escape there.'

Hector frowned. I hadn't meant to remind him of the bookshelf fiasco.

'What's more, the post-mortem result has now come through. As Norman was apparently the only person on the bus known to have a serious grudge against her, they considered him a prime suspect and have arrested him on suspicion of murder.'

I thought back. 'But I don't remember him having any

contact with her on the bus. In fact, he was trying not even to make eye contact with anyone. It was as if he didn't want anyone to notice him, which was a bit optimistic, given he's a bit hulking.'

Hector shrugged. 'Well, someone must have reported that he did. Maybe the bus driver saw something that you missed. He'd be able to see everything that was going on inside the bus, with the combination of his rear-view mirror and onboard CCTV.'

'I can't pretend I'm not disappointed,' I replied. 'I thought underneath all his bluster, he was a decent chap. Or at least I had no reason to think he wasn't.'

'So, I guess it's case closed, sweetheart,' said Hector gently. 'Sorry to thwart your sleuthing instincts when you're just getting stuck in, but I suppose we should feel grateful for once that the police have beaten you to it.'

I heaved myself up out of the armchair. 'I need a drink,' I said, heading for the fridge. 'Unlike someone I could name, I didn't start early. So what was the cause of death in the end? Did Bob say?'

Hector followed me into the kitchen. 'Believe it or not, the kids were right, so at least they'll be pleased.'

I stopped in my tracks, my hand on the fridge door. 'What, she was killed by swallowing chewing gum? Come to think of it, I noticed both Norman and the bus driver were chewing gum. Don't tell me he forced chewing gum on her?'

Hector fetched a pair of wine glasses from the cupboard. 'Not chewing gum, Sophie. Poison.'

'Poison? Really? What sort?'

Hector shook his head. 'It's not yet been made public knowledge, presumably because it might hamper their investigation. I'm not sure Bob should even have told me that much, but he was looking pretty shaken up by it all, and I think he needed to offload to help himself deal with it. I think he's distantly related to the Boggins family, so it feels more personal to him. Just because he's a police officer doesn't mean he's immune to the shock of it, any more than we are. He's not part of the local Murder Investigation Team. I think at the moment he mostly works in traffic.'

'But who poisoned her and with what? If the police aren't going to tell us, I'm going to do my best to find out by other means.'

23

THE EMPTY BUS

It was therefore with mixed feelings that I set off for my intensive driving course the next day. Part of me wanted to stay in Wendlebury, so that I could continue investigating Janice's murder, and the other half couldn't wait to leave.

I had to be in Dorset for my first driving lesson at midday, which meant catching the commuter bus from Wendlebury to Slate Green, then another bus from Slate Green to Bath, then a train from Bath. Expecting the buses to be crowded, I was travelling light. I was only going to be away for three nights, after all. I executed a masterful piece of packing, rolling rather than folding items of clothing to make them fit into the smallest possible space, and taking just my laptop and e-reader rather than the pile of paperbacks on my nightstand. I managed to fit everything into a neat, rectangular bag small enough to qualify as hand luggage on an aircraft, chosen in this case to fit easily into the little luggage space behind the bus-driver's cab, just in front of the fateful seat where Janice Boggins had come to her unfortunate end. As I closed the zip, I hoped I wouldn't have to sit in that same seat. I determined to arrive at the bus stop early to be near the front of the queue.

I left Hector asleep in my bed. I'd made sure the night before that the alarm on his phone was set to wake him in time to open the bookshop for nine o'clock.

After a last cuddle with Blossom, whom Joshua had again kindly agreed to feed while I was away, I tiptoed to the front door and opened it as quietly as possible so as not to disturb Hector. As I headed for my garden gate, I heard a tapping at the window behind me. I thought for a moment it was Hector reminding me of something I'd forgotten, such as my phone charger. I turned and discovered the sound was coming from next door. Joshua, already up and dressed, moustache and hair immaculate, was waving me off. I hoped he didn't go in to feed Blossom until after Hector had gone to work. I hadn't mentioned he'd be staying over, and I didn't want Joshua to mistake him for a burglar.

As I strolled up to the bus stop, the air was damp and chilly, but refreshing, albeit with a hint of decay. The coppery fallen leaves scattered on the pavement were slippery underfoot and I trod carefully to avoid falling over. Having mustered my courage to book this driving course, I didn't want to spoil my plans at the last minute by twisting an ankle or breaking a wrist.

A few villagers passing by in their cars waved to me in greeting. Most of the cars bore two or three passengers. I hadn't realised so many villagers now lift-shared, but then I wasn't normally out and about early enough to see the morning commuter traffic.

As the bus stop came into view, I realised why there were so many car shares. Not another soul was at the bus stop. I checked my watch. Had I set my alarm wrong? Had the clocks changed overnight to Greenwich Mean Time without me remembering to adjust my clocks? In that case, it would be an hour earlier than I thought, and the bus would not be due for another hour.

Then I remembered the clocks only ever change in the early hours on a Sunday morning, so that couldn't be the case. Also, I'd checked the time on my watch the day before against the pips on the six o'clock news on the radio, so I knew it was spot on.

Still bewildered, I perched on the narrow bench in the bus shelter and set my bag on my lap. Suddenly aware of being watched, I glanced across to the village shop and saw Carol staring at me. As soon as she'd got my attention, she came out from behind the counter and made for the shop door. She opened it and stood on the threshold, speaking to me across the street in a stage whisper.

'I think they're all too scared, Sophie.'

I shook my head, not understanding. 'Who?'

'Everybody.'

'Scared of what?'

'Of travelling on the bus. Since the unfortunate incident on Friday. You know what I mean.'

I certainly did.

'But didn't you hear?' I hissed back. 'She died of poisoning. It's not infectious. It's not like she had the plague. Other passengers won't die just by sitting in her seat.'

Even so, I was relieved when a double-decker turned up instead of the single-decker in which Janice had died. The driver, however, was the same – Norman Arch's replacement.

'Only me today, I'm afraid,' I said to the driver as I climbed the steps.

After staring at me for a moment without replying, chomping on his chewing gum, I realised he couldn't hear me because of the earbuds in his ears. I tapped my ear to remind him, and grudgingly he moved one about a centimetre from his ear.

'I'm sorry, it's just me today,' I said as I fumbled in my purse for coins. 'All your usual passengers seem to have cadged lifts.'

He shrugged. Considering he was the driver who had found Janice dead on Friday, he was remarkably calm.

As I counted out the coins on the little black plastic tray between us, he blew a small bubble with his gum, let it pop and sucked it back in. After moving it across to one side of his mouth to make a bump in his cheek like an inverted dimple, he deigned to reply.

'Hardly helping the cause to save the number 27, are they? I heard you lot had all pledged to pile on here every day to convince Highwayman to keep it going.'

When he peered sardonically over his shoulder at the empty bus, I had a sudden urge to buy twenty tickets, to fool the bus company into thinking there'd been a huge demand this morning. Then I remembered the onboard CCTV system. I'd be fooling no one except myself.

While the machine printed my ticket, the driver took the wodge of gum out of his mouth, looked at it, then stuck it onto a corner of the rear-view mirror. For a moment I thought he was saving it for later, then realised that there was no other receptacle within his reach in which to dispose of it.

The layout of the double-decker was entirely different from the usual 27. To make the most of the opportunity for a scenic view of the fields en route, I headed upstairs to the very front seat. I sat on the left for the best view, but as the lanes are mostly single track, with just a few passing places, it didn't make much difference – I'd see very little tarmac either side.

As the bus lurched into action and up the High Street, I had to admire the surly driver's skill as he navigated around parked cars and turned onto the country lane. I hoped for his sake we didn't meet any traffic coming towards us, though given the size of the bus, most vehicles would have to give way, being more manoeuvrable. What would happen if we encountered a tractor or a supermarket delivery van? I spent the rest of the journey to Slate Green devising a country lane Top Trumps – tractor: 95 points for size, 5 points for size of turning circle, and so on. I rather enjoyed my solitary state, pretending the bus driver was my chauffeur and I was an eccentric billionaire who preferred buses to Bentleys. Later it came as a shock to change onto the Bath bus at Slate Green, which was full. I just wished the 27 had been as popular.

24

DRIVEN AWAY

After spending the morning in big buses and trains, climbing into a small hatchback at the driving school felt claustrophobic, and it took me a while to attune to the feel of its pedals, so different to those in Saxon Arch's car, and even less like the controls of the Land Rover. However, my instructor was positive and encouraging, keeping up a running commentary of what I should be doing and the impact on the car, so that by the end of the first day, I understood the purpose of the clutch so well that I almost felt I could have stripped the engine down and installed a new one. Having practised on all gears, including reverse, I was pleased with my progress, but mentally drained, and ready to spend a quiet evening in my budget hotel, picnicking on snacks bought from the nearest supermarket and drinking tea made with the tiny kettle provided in my room.

Before long, I began to feel lonely, missing the comforting mass of a warm cat asleep on my lap, and a warm man at my side. Oh, and Hector's conversation.

I called him to tell him I thought I'd done well so far, meeting the milestones expected by the end of the first day, which gave me confidence the week would be well spent. Only just before I rang off did I remember to tell him about the empty commuter bus.

'Kind of ironic that they sent a double-decker,' I added.

'The police will have impounded the usual bus while they investigate Janice's murder,' he replied. 'You know, dusting it for fingerprints, and so on.'

'And traces of the fatal poison,' I added. 'By the way, I thought of Sina's theory when I was speaking to the driver. He just kept chewing his gum without speaking, and staring at me, like a cow chewing the cud, but less attractive. I know we haven't exactly made a friend of Norman Arch, but I can tell you I'd rather be driven by Norman than his replacement any day. This man was so sullen and a real slob. Do you know, he stuck his chewing gum on his rear-view mirror when he'd finished with it.'

Hector made a suitably disgusted noise. 'If I were Janice Boggins, the sight of him doing that would have put me right off my picnic.'

'Me too,' I replied. 'Anyway, let's not get distracted. What we need to find out now is who administered the poison to Mrs Boggins.'

'And how,' added Hector.

I considered for a moment. 'I only saw her tucking into the picnic she'd brought with her. She'd hardly pack her own picnic with toxic snacks. Assuming of course that she packed her own picnic.'

'What a shame this didn't happen on a plane,' mused Hector. 'Then they would have asked if she'd packed her own bag.'

I laughed. 'It is hard to imagine someone forcing poison on her on the bus, though. Not even the burly Norman Arch, even though he could easily have overpowered her physically. There wasn't much of her.' I sighed. 'I wish I hadn't come here now. I feel so useless here, miles away from the scene of the crime.'

As ever, Hector always knew the right thing to say. 'Actually, getting a bit of distance from the situation, literally as well as metaphorically, might help you puzzle it out, rather than if you were here. It's not as if there are physical clues you can examine here, with the police having impounded the bus. It's all just talk and idle chatter, which is a distraction rather than a help. There's been no end of gossip about it in the shop today. I suppose it helps people process the tragedy. It's a shock to lose a member of our village community so unnecessarily like that.'

'You're right. Oh well, perhaps if I sleep on it, I'll wake up with a ready-made solution in my head in the morning.'

'That often happens to me with a plot point in my novels,' said Hector. 'If I make sure the last thing I think about before I go to sleep is whatever I've got stuck over, it all falls into place by morning.'

'What a good thing you're not here to distract me either,' I teased him. 'I'll see what I can do.'

25

THE AMPHIBIOUS BUS RIDES AGAIN

Despite my best efforts, the only vision that came to me in the night was of myself driving a bus through various terrains, from up and down hairpin bends to surfing tsunamis.

'Ah, Carol's amphibious bus!' I exclaimed as I made myself a cup of coffee with the tiny hotel kettle. You could always depend on Carol to mangle the English language at least once in every conversation. For once, I wasn't sure what she really meant by it.

But as I was driving around the local roads during my lessons that day, learning to negotiate bends and traffic lights and roundabouts, my dream kept coming back to me. This was more helpful than it sounds, because by contrast, normal roads now seemed relatively easy to drive on, especially under the instruction of the calm and unflappable Mick, a forty-something with prematurely white hair.

When I returned to my room that evening, I couldn't rest until I'd googled 'amphibious bus', which got me no closer to understanding Carol's meaning. Then I realised adding 'High-wayman Leif Oakham' might help. Sure enough, up he popped in a publicity shot showing a smart new bus parked on a wide tarmac three-laned carriageway, but with no other cars in sight. Arching above it was a motorway-style gantry bearing directional signage to places I'd never heard of. In the background was a post-apocalyptic array of wrecked buildings. What was the bus doing there? I couldn't see a bus stop, nor imagine anyone living there.

I clicked on the image to reveal a few paragraphs of explanatory text, which began:

Highwayman CEO Leif Oakham takes a trial trip on his company's new experimental bus service, currently being put through its paces at the National Fire Service Training College, Moreton-in-Marsh.

That explained the burned-out hotel and warehouse in the background. The lifelike carriageway, free of other traffic, must have made the perfect test site for a driverless bus. I kept reading.

The gloves are off now to see which bus service will be the first to pilot the proposed autonomous electric passenger service designed specifically for country lanes. Crafty cost-cutting like this will keep public transport ticking over for the foreseeable future, if only the tricky technology can be proven to keep the vehicles on the track.

Avoid alliteration, I wanted to say to the journalist.

So, if Highwayman wanted to be first to launch such a scheme, which other companies were in the running? I hadn't heard of another bus service looking to take over the 27 route when Highwayman pulled out. Then I remembered at the special parish council meeting, someone had alluded to a dirty tricks campaign by a rival company. Leif Oakham had refused to be drawn, whether due to personal decency and professionalism or awareness of the rules of libel. But I began to wonder whether there might be something in the heckler's theory after all.

A search for other bus companies in the South West brought up at the top of the list GB Bus and Coach, run by one Gavin Bing, who had just marked his thirtieth anniversary as its chief executive. That must mean he was close to retirement age or even past it, unlike the dashing Leif Oakham. When I clicked on the image tab, I discovered a photo of Bing standing proudly beside a gleaming black Tesla with a personalised licence plate.

I swear for a moment my heart stopped beating. The licence plate was the same as on the car whose passenger stopped to talk to Janice Boggins: GB 123.

I opened a new window on my laptop and searched for the GB Bus and Coach company. It wasn't a name I'd come across locally. I'd never seen a bus with that firm's livery at the Slate Green bus depot. The 'find us' section of their website told me why. Their head office was in Casterbridge, Dorset. The South West was a big region, encompassing everywhere from the Cotswolds to Cornwall, from Weston-super-Mare to Wessex. Highwayman could well consider a company based in Caster-bridge as a rival looking to poach its Cotswold territory.

I wondered how far I was from Casterbridge now. I hadn't noticed it as a station stop on the train on my way down, but if I drove back, would it be on my way? Searching on Google Maps, I found it was just a few minutes' drive from my hotel.

I'd already promised myself that if I passed my test that Thursday, I'd buy a car to drive home, provided the garage had something I liked at a fair price. Now I made another pledge: in my new car, I'd detour to visit GB Bus and Coach's headquarters.

I wasn't sure how I'd manage it yet, but somehow, I wanted to find out why Gavin Bing had been making small talk with passengers waiting for the 27 bus in Wendlebury Barrow when it was way off his patch.

I had just two days in between times to dream up a pretext to get Gavin Bing to see me. I was confident I'd think of something. While the practical part of my brain was focusing on getting the mechanics of driving right, my analytical brain would be left to its own devices. But the most important thing now was to pass my driving test on Thursday.

26

PUT TO THE TEST

I decided not to confide my plan in Hector just yet, but to focus on my driving course.

After spending all day Wednesday and Thursday morning practising manoeuvres, I was looking forward to my test in the quiet streets of the little market town of Casterbridge. My confidence faded once I was sitting beside the examiner, a stern, elderly chap with the severe hairline of a monk's tonsure. I tried not to think about my recent discovery that monks wore their hair in that style not for religious reasons, but to reduce nit infestation. Whatever happened, I shouldn't take my hands off the wheel to scratch my head.

'Get a move on!' he cried, at one point, as I took my time pulling out to overtake a milk float. That seemed needlessly cruel. I wasn't going to let this guy push me around, just because he had a licence, and I didn't.

'I'm sorry, but I'm not going to overtake unless I can see the amount of road clear that I need to complete the manoeuvre,' I said. 'And I can see the road ahead better than you can from the passenger seat.'

'When I hit the dashboard with my pen, you're to do an emergency stop,' he announced a few minutes later as we reached a clear, straight stretch of road.

I glanced in my rear-view mirror. 'Well, don't do it just yet, or that idiot who is far too close to my back bumper will go piling straight into me.'

His pen was already in mid-air when he glanced at the wing mirror on his side of the car.

'Next left,' he barked.

Our follower carried on down the main road. In the side street we'd turned into, there were no moving vehicles in front or behind us, only parked cars on either side.

'Okay,' he murmured, and tapped the dashboard.

I slammed my feet so hard on the clutch and brake that he lurched forward and fell back hard against his seat.

'Full marks for reaction time,' he conceded, rubbing the back of his head where it had collided with the head restraint. Just as well the head restraint was there, or his head might have ricocheted off the parcel shelf.

Finally, he commanded me to pull into the test centre car park and pointed to an empty space. Although I could more easily have driven straight into it, I showed off by reversing neatly in. I wanted to make him feel bad for having failed me.

'Well, Miss Sayers.' He played for time, lifting the mark sheet on his clipboard to rifle for something underneath it. I assumed it was a claim form for my refund from the driving school. 'I'm pleased to tell you that you're now a qualified driver. Here is your voucher for ten per cent off the purchase price of any second-hand vehicle priced five thousand pounds or above from the car showroom next door. They can also arrange your insurance at a discount so you can drive away in your new car today.'

I took the voucher with both hands and gaped at it.

'But when you told me to get a move on with overtaking that milk float, I was sure I'd failed,' I said.

He unclipped his seat belt and turned to face me for the first time. Now I could see he had a playful twinkle in his dark brown eyes and dimples at the corners of his mouth.

'Miss Sayers, I knew from the moment we pulled away that unless you collided with something or knocked someone down – in which case I'd have no choice but to fail you – that you were a competent, confident driver. Otherwise, I'd never have shouted at you. Congratulations. Now on you go.'

I couldn't help wondering whether a female examiner would have been so presumptuous.

But I'd passed my test, I could choose a new car – and then I could be on my way to GB Bus and Coach.

27

FOUR WHEELS GOOD

Clutching the driving school's discount voucher, I entered the salesroom of the affiliated garage next door. A beaming young man in an ostentatiously smart-casual combination of chinos and linen shirt got up from his desk to welcome me, while also walking slightly crablike towards the end of the showroom that housed the more expensive models.

I returned his broad smile, while heading in the opposite direction, mentally prepared not to be manipulated into buying something out of my price range.

Conscious that the special offer might be artificial – that the showroom prices might just be inflated by ten per cent to give buyers the illusion they were getting a deep discount – I'd spent the previous evening doing some homework in my hotel room. I'd looked up the details of all the cars that I could afford in their current stock, and checked out the prices, comparing like with like at other dealers. To my surprise, their prices seemed only slightly higher than average, so my promised discount still proved a good deal.

'I'm after something boxy and practical for transporting

stock for my business,' I said, feeling rather grand. I decided not to disclose the nature of that business. He didn't look like the type to value books. 'Economical with fuel and spacious inside without too big a footprint for parking, nor with a massive turning circle. I live in the countryside, and my home village is approached through single-track lanes.'

He nodded. 'Good choice, madame.'

'I was thinking of a Fiat Panda or a Nissan Cube,' I said, before he could suggest anything flashier. 'Lots of boot space in both, I believe. Maximum budget is five K.'

I hoped saying 'five K' like that rather than 'five thousand' would make me sound like an experienced wheeler-dealer, rather than the nervous first-car buyer that I was in reality.

I allowed him to lead me out of the showroom and into the car park, where a row of used cars was parked in a sunburst pattern, the cars radiating bonnet first around a large half-moon of flowerbed.

'Sure you wouldn't prefer a Fiat 500? Stylish, nippy little numbers, very popular with the ladies. We have some nearly new models here.'

I gritted my teeth. Next, he'd be recommending cars with 'only one previous careful lady driver'.

'No, I'm particularly interested in your Pandas.'

That didn't sound quite so businesslike, and I suppressed a giggle.

He let out a sigh and raised his hands in surrender. 'I'm so sorry, madame, you've just missed the opportunity to snap up a lovely Tuscany Green number we let go this morning. Perfect for motoring about country lanes. Blends in a treat.'

Honestly, who thinks up these names? I hoped he didn't think I was one of those women drivers whose first priority is colour.

'What about that one over there?' I pointed to a Panda the shade of a satsuma.

'Ah, Sicilian Orange,' he cooed. 'Good choice, madame. Easy to find in a car park.'

If I hadn't been so eager to drive myself home in celebration of passing my test, I would probably have turned my back and stalked out at that point. Instead, I summoned up a few technical questions that my dad had primed me to ask when I consulted him the previous evening. I was pleased when the salesman hesitated, having to look up the answers in the car's handbook.

'Perhaps you'd like to try a short test-drive?' he suggested, opening the driver's door for me.

I slid into the seat, rested my feet on the pedals, and my hands at a perfect ten-to-two on the steering wheel.

'It does come with a guarantee, doesn't it?' I queried quickly. I really didn't want to have to demonstrate my driving prowess in the company of this condescending man.

He nodded. 'Yes, of course, madame. As I'm sure the driving school explained to you.'

I slapped the steering wheel decisively, then climbed out of the car. 'Then I'm sure it'll be fine. I'll take it, please.'

'Good choice, madame. Now, if you'd like to follow me, I'll take care of your paperwork.'

'I like you to arrange discounted insurance too, please,' I added, before I could be tempted to change my mind.

I lingered for a moment as he strolled back to the showroom, just long enough to pat my new possession affectionately on the bonnet.

'Hello, Tiger Lily,' I whispered. 'You and I are going to have fun. But first, I'd better phone Hector to tell him our good news.'

28

IN THE DRIVING SEAT

There was a certain irony in my first journey in my new car being to a bus company's headquarters.

As I was pulling into the visitors' car park, I decided to pose as a relation of Janice Boggins, needing closure on her death for the sake of her family. I would ask what she'd said to him because those may have been her last words. Their conversation might indicate how she was feeling – whether she was feeling ill from natural causes, or showed symptoms of poisoning, or, heaven forbid, that she had been planning to take her own life on the bus as an extreme form of protest against the cuts. I closed my eyes to block out that awful idea.

Surely that would make him open up to me. He probably didn't even know she had died at all, never mind in suspicious circumstances. Why would he? He lived too far from Wendlebury for the village grapevine to reach him, and the police hadn't yet released the story to the media, presumably because they feared it might hamper their investigation, so it hadn't made regional or national headlines. If he had any decency, he'd treat me kindly out of sympathy. I couldn't see why he wouldn't believe me – unless someone else who knew me happened to be there, to give the game away.

Norman Arch, perhaps? Was this story that he was visiting his sister in Dorset a front for coming to visit GB Bus and Coach to plead for a job? Not that these two circumstances need to be mutually exclusive. But even if that was his intention, there was no way he'd be here to rat on me now, as he was currently in police custody.

As I locked my car and turned to face the main building, I spotted a sleek, top-of-the-range electric car plugged into a charging station in a parking space reserved for... GB 123. Its green light winked at me in the late afternoon gloom. Hurrah! If the car was there, Gavin Bing must be on the premises.

Taking a deep breath for courage, I strode up the steps to the entrance, moving quickly before I could lose my nerve. The motion-sensitive double glass doors swung open noiselessly as I approached. I'd been expecting them to emit the distinctive hydraulic huff of bus doors.

Inside, the reception area had been designed to glorify the golden age of the public bus before car ownership became so widespread. The sofas for waiting visitors were in the same style as the bench seats on vintage buses, their prickly, stiff tartan velour presumably chosen not to show the dirt. Adorning the walls were vintage posters advertising days out by bus to heritage sites and seaside resorts. Beneath the glass top of the coffee table were displays of old bus tickets and ticket machines, among artfully scattered pre-decimal coins. This nostalgic display was a great way to build visitors' affection for public buses, warming them up for any business they were about to do with GB Bus and Coach. But it was also terribly dated, the body language of a once-great company that preferred looking back to the glory days of public transport, rather than looking forward to conquer industry challenges in the twenty-first century, such as environmental issues and soaring costs.

I headed for the reception desk, a sturdy old-fashioned oak double pedestal. It was the kind that might have graced a bank manager's office in those heady days when a day out by bus cost pennies. The disadvantage of this picturesque set-up was that it put whatever work the receptionist was doing on display, rather than shielding her from the public.

The receptionist, who looked about fifty, stood out against the muted tones of the décor in a too-tight cerise nylon suit and frilly lemon blouse. As I approached, she looked up, and I forced my most winning smile, tempered with a hint of mournfulness.

'Hello there, I'm sorry to trouble you, but I'm the niece of the late Janice Boggins.'

The woman furrowed her crookedly pencilled eyebrows and gave a slight shake of her head. 'I'm sorry, should I know her? Did she used to work for us?'

I closed my eyes and put a hand to my temple to suggest my grief was so fresh that it pained me to think of her.

'No, but I believe your boss did, and he heard her last words, before she so sadly passed away. My family and I would be so grateful if Mr Bing could kindly tell us what they were. It will help us come to terms with our sad loss.' I staggered slightly and rested my hand on the edge of her desk, as if to steady myself, unbalanced by the weight of my fresh grief.

The woman's eyes widened, perhaps anxious that I might be about to fall to the floor in a dead faint. 'So, Gavin – Mr Bing – was a friend of hers?'

I opened one eye. 'In a way. You see, he spoke to her before she caught her final bus.'

The woman put her head on one side. 'Is that a euphemism?'

'No,' I said quickly, having to grit my teeth to prevent myself from laughing.

When she jotted a note in shorthand on her pad, I noticed an extraordinarily large diamond ring on her wedding finger, but no accompanying wedding band. I bet that got in the way when she was doing her filing.

'No, she was literally about to board the bus in our village, up in the Cotswolds, when he stopped to speak to her. We would love to know whether he thought she looked unwell. She'd been in such good health that her death came out of the blue. Maybe he can tell us something that might help us discover the cause of her death – a piercing headache heralding a fatal stroke, perhaps, or a crushing pain in her chest and left arm that might indicate a heart attack. As her death was unexpected, there will have to be a post-mortem. It could be weeks before we know the cause of death, and they won't release her body for a funeral until then either. In the meantime, it would make such a difference to my uncle, her poor widower, especially, to know Mr Bing's opinion.'

The woman wrapped her arms about herself in a comforting hug. I'd lucked out here – she was dripping in empathy.

'That must be hard,' she said.

I pulled a tissue from my pocket and dabbed at my eyes.

'So where did Gavin – Mr Bing – meet her if she lived in the Cotswolds? We don't run any bus services there, although I know he'd like to. It's a beautiful part of the country.'

'Yes.' I was glad to have common ground that we might bond over. 'And my aunt was born and bred there. Her dying wish was that her ashes should be scattered along the part of the Cotswold Way that runs through our village.'

The woman drew back slightly. 'Oh, so were those her last words?'

Bother! I was such a bad liar.

'Oh no, what I mean is, she'd put that in her will years ago. We all thought it would be very many years before we had to act upon them. Although it will still be, if we must wait for the post-mortem.'

She picked up her shorthand pad and pen. 'What was your auntie's name again?'

'Janice Boggins,' I said quickly before she could change her mind.

She stuck her pencil through her straggly silver French pleat and rolled back her chair, slipping shiny court shoes carefully over her bunions before getting to her feet.

'Well, Mr Bing's a very busy man, always driving out and about all over the place to keep an eye on his bus empire, but I'll pop my head round his door now and ask him whether he has any recollection of your auntie.' She gave a proud smile. 'I may only be a receptionist, but Mr B never minds me popping in to see him. While I'm gone, do you mind signing the visitors' book, please?'

She opened a large hardback book that sat on a corner of her desk and turned it round to face me, offering a red pen bearing the GB Bus and Coach company name and logo. Then she got up to peer in the full-length mirror on the wall to one side of her desk, primping her dishevelled hair with her fingertips and pulling at her clingy pencil skirt in an attempt to hide the visible lines of her underwear.

'What did you say your name was again?'

'Boggins,' I replied, very glad that it wasn't. 'Martha Boggins.'

'Just a mo,' she replied. 'Bear with.'

The tapping of her court shoe heels faded into the distance down a long corridor.

I laid down the pen, wondering why she hadn't just phoned him. Maybe she hadn't really gone to consult him at all, but to call security. Or perhaps she didn't want me to hear how she described me. I sidestepped to glimpse myself in her mirror. I was looking perfectly respectable. I had nothing to be embarrassed about.

Perhaps she just liked any excuse to chat up her boss, even though he must have been well past his prime, having just celebrated his thirtieth year as CEO. But I suppose his position would make him rich and powerful still. That would explain the preening before she went to see him.

Meanwhile, ever curious, I flicked back a couple of pages of the visitors' book, interested to see whether anyone famous had been there lately. As I closed the book and placed it back on her desk, I took the opportunity of being left alone to take a sneaky peek at whatever she was working on. It looked for all the world as if she was preparing wedding party favours, tying red, white and blue striped ribbons around the gathered tops of white net bags of sugared almonds. I'd noticed she was wearing a flashy engagement ring on her expensively manicured hand. Perhaps she was engaged to Gavin Bing? Was another late-in-life wedding on the cards, like Carol and Ted's? That would explain why he was allowing her to prepare stuff for her wedding – their wedding – during the working day. If so, best of luck to them. It's never too late to find love.

Just then, a dark-haired man, perhaps in his early forties, entered the reception area through the front door behind me, and I stepped back from the desk, hoping he hadn't noticed me prying. A light breeze followed him, sharp enough to lift a sheet of paper off the reception desk. When it drifted through the air to land at my feet, I bent to pick it up. At first glance, I assumed the list of names and addresses was the future Mrs Bing's wedding guest list. But as I was returning it to the desk, I realised the names weren't of people, but of places. There were no contact numbers or email addresses either, nor names or numbers of houses, just streets, village names and postcodes. That narrowed the location down to a handful of buildings at least. A different time of day was noted against each line.

Halfway down the list was High Street, Wendlebury Barrow, along with the postcode of the village shop – just one character different from the postcodes of my cottage and of Hector's House. I scanned the rest of the list.

Noticing that the breeze had blown the list off a stack of photocopies, I hoped the receptionist wouldn't miss the copy in my hand. The new arrival in reception had headed for the lift. He was now standing with his back to me, watching the indicator board as the lift descended. Quickly I folded the sheet and slipped it into my jacket pocket unseen.

The tapping of the receptionist's shoes echoed at the far end of the corridor, and I realised my prying time would be cut short.

As I stepped back from her desk and averted my gaze from her work, I noticed a pile of boxes beside it. One was a case of self-heating coffee tins, plus there were various snack foods. The biggest box contained a dozen Henley wicker hampers, the label told me, measuring 8cm x 20cm x 30cm. Handy size for one person, I thought. Just right for... for Janice Boggins to take on the bus!

So, Janice hadn't packed her own snacks, as she usually did. She was tucking into a basket of treats presented to her by Gavin Bing.

But I had no time to find out what the other items destined

to go in the hampers were. The receptionist was marching towards me, all smiles, pink-cheeked, and with her low-cut blouse now slightly untucked. I stepped back from her desk and resumed my grief-stricken niece persona.

The receptionist gave me a sympathetic smile, suitably tinged with sadness.

'Gavin – Mr Bing – says he's sorry for your loss, but he doesn't remember speaking to your aunt.'

Remembering my charade, I put one hand over my eyes.

'Oh, that is a blow,' I said, my voice breaking with emotion. 'But you have been so kind. Everyone has been so kind about Auntie Janice.'

My performance so far had impressed me. I wondered whether to audition for the next Wendlebury Players' drama production.

I'd moved the receptionist too.

'And there's you having come all the way from – where did you say it was again?'

It dawned on me that if Bing was denying knowledge of meeting Janice, perhaps it was because he never asked her name. But if he was somehow implicated in her death, it would be safer not to mention where I lived. What if he wanted me silenced?

'Oh, just a little place you won't have heard of,' I said lightly. 'A little village called Hawkesbury Upton in the Cotswolds.'

Her sympathetic gaze transmuted into puzzled concern, and I saw her glance at her list. Then she coughed. 'Sorry, never heard of it. But I bet it's lovely with a pretty name like that.'

I retrieved my tissue to dab my eyes again, almost dislodging the folded piece of paper secreted in my pocket. I turned my gasp of horror at nearly giving my theft away into a choking sob of grief.

'Yes, and I wouldn't want to live anywhere else. Especially now dear Auntie Janice will be buried there.'

If Mrs Boggins had been in her grave already, she'd have been pirouetting at my lies. Remembering that my real aunt, Great Auntie May, lay in Wendlebury churchyard enabled me to wring out real tears.

'Here,' said the receptionist, picking up a bag of sugared almonds by its ribbon and holding it out to me. 'Have one of these for your journey home. Sugar's good for grief. And they'll be delicious. I haven't tried them myself as I'm on a diet, but Mr B insists on only the best for the goody bags he uses for PR and stuff. These little hampers are for his "Shop by Bus" campaign that's running just now. He's been giving them at random to people at bus stops all over the place. Isn't he sweet? He's like that, you know. Always thinking of his customers.'

I gave a watery smile as I slipped the net of sweets into my handbag.

'You're very kind too,' I said, meaning it. 'Although I feel I'm getting these under false pretences. I came here by car, not bus.'

She smiled. 'Don't worry. It'll be our little secret. Safe journey home and may your auntie RIP.'

She said the letters R-I-P, rather than saying the words 'rest in peace', and I forced a smile of thanks before heading swiftly back to the car park.

For a moment, I looked around for Hector's Land Rover, forgetting I'd driven myself here. Then I remembered I was now the proud owner of a car – but could I remember the licence plate? Nope. Just as well I'd chosen such a brightly coloured vehicle.

Easy to find in a car park, the salesman had said, and he was right.

'You okay, love?' called a deep voice from the corner of the car park. A stocky man with a broken nose and cauliflower ears was leaning on the open driver's door of the GB 123 car, swinging his chauffeur's cap from one hand. 'Sorry, do I know you?'

He stared at my chest. I hoped that meant he was looking for a visitor's badge for security reasons.

'I'm Martha Boggins,' I said firmly, reaching in my handbag for my keys as I headed for Tiger Lily. 'And I'm fine, thank you. I'm just leaving.' My broad smile reflecting my relief, I took a few steps towards the right car. 'Although it would be really handy if you could give me some directions.'

Tiger Lily was too old to come with a built-in satnav, and I hadn't had time yet to buy a dashboard mount to use my phone as one. I turned back to the chauffeur.

'Could you please tell me the best way to get to Wendlebury Barrow from here?' So much for not revealing where I lived. Still, I had to find my way home. But perhaps I could distract him with a different place name. 'No, silly question,' I continued. 'You won't have heard of it. But if you could point me towards Chipping Sodbury, that would get me nearly there. Everyone has heard of Chipping Sodbury.'

The man donned his cap and stood up a little straighter. 'I can tell you how to get anywhere, love. I'm a walking satnav, I am.'

I grinned.

'That's a handy superpower.' I swung my keys from my fingertip. 'Can you do that for any place name? How do I get to Drumnadrochit?'

Not that I had any intention of going there – it was just one of my favourite Scottish place names.

'Take the first left at the end of the road,' he began, deadpan, before breaking into a hearty laugh. 'No idea, darlin'. Sorry, I'm having you on. I just happened to be up Wendlebury Barrow way last week, so it's front of my mind.'

'Thank you very much,' I said when he had finished directing me. He couldn't have known what I was really thanking him for, was his admission that Gavin Bing was now a suspect in the murder of Janice Boggins – one that the official Murder Investigation Team had completely missed.

29

ON THE ROAD

Driving out of the car park under the bemused scrutiny of the chauffeur took all my concentration. It wasn't until I'd navigated onto a quiet, wide road that cut across the Dorset countryside towards home that I had the headspace to reflect on what I'd learned at GB Bus and Coach.

First, I was now convinced that either the receptionist was romantically involved with Gavin Bing or admired him from afar, which might encourage her to cover for him if he was doing something illegal. Second, I was now pretty sure that Gavin Bing's chauffeur had driven him to Wendlebury Barrow.

It didn't necessarily follow that his passenger was Bing, but if I showed Carol a photo of Gavin Bing, she might be able to confirm whether he was the man she saw talking to Janice at the bus stop that morning. For my present purposes, it made sense to assume it was him unless, or until, proven otherwise. I planned to call Detective Inspector Easterbrook who had taken my statement to give him this additional information the minute I got home. If I hadn't left his card at home in my cottage, I'd have phoned him straight away.

Although for a probationer, I felt reasonably confident driving, the intense concentration required to get me through the course was now catching up with me, and suddenly I was overcome with exhaustion. I decided to stop for a restorative cup of coffee at the first opportunity.

When a sign for services loomed ahead, I mentally prepared myself to leave the main carriageway at the slip road. I was certainly getting plenty of practice at manoeuvring on my first day as a qualified driver and car owner.

I slowed down, ready to turn off, to the annoyance of the powder-blue car behind me. The driver pulled out sharply, only to be tooted at by a darker, larger car coming up behind him at a speed that must have been way over the limit. I hoped the blue car's driver felt chastened for being so intolerant of me. Only after both cars were blurry dots in the distance did I realise I'd braked far too early for the turn-off. I made a mental note next time to slow down only at the three-hundred-yard sign: blue with three white slashes.

As I applied the handbrake, I realised my mouth was unbearably dry – perhaps a by-product of the tension of my visit to GB Bus and Coach in between my first two solo stints at driving. I was tempted to pop one of the sugared almonds in my mouth, but, glancing at the gauze bag at the top of my handbag, I realised what a nice thank-you present the sweets would make either for Mrs Wetherley for filling in for me again at the tearoom, or for Hector, because I knew he was fond of nuts, though preferring the savoury, spicy sort rather than the sugar-coated. I decided to save them.

A few minutes later, as I climbed back into the car – the only bright orange Panda in the car park, not surprisingly – I jolted my takeaway cup on the steering wheel, and a few drops splattered onto its shiny leather cover. With pride of ownership, I was more concerned for the pristine appearance of my new car, rather than the lost mouthful of coffee. I reached into my jacket pocket for a tissue to wipe it clean. As I pulled out the tissue, the folded sheet of paper I'd stolen from the receptionist's deck came with it. I dropped it onto my lap, wiped the steering wheel clean, and disposed of the damp brown tissue in my handbag.

For safety's sake, I decided I'd better drink my coffee while stationary, even though I was pleased to remember there were two cup-holders conveniently positioned between the front seats. A good sound system, adequate boot space for boxes of books, and cup holders had all been top of my wish-list for my first car.

My first sip told me the coffee needed to cool for a minute, so to pass the time, I unfolded the paper on my lap and began reading, trying to find a reason that Wendlebury Barrow High Street would be listed without anyone's name.

I scanned the list of place names – all tiny villages, many with double-barrelled names like Wendlebury Barrow's, and, I now realised, all in the Cotswolds. Still feeling clever after passing my test, I was sure if I thought hard enough, I'd spot a common thread.

And so I did. When I spotted the names of two other local villages on the list, the first thing I pictured was their bus stops. On board the bus, I'd waited at both of them for fellow passengers to board or disembark before my journey could continue.

The nearest to me was St Bride's Lane, which passes the gated entrance to the girls' boarding school, also named St Bride's. I'd once alighted there to take afternoon tea with my friend, Gemma Lamb, their English teacher. A long private drive runs from the school gates to the forecourt of the main school building, and it had taken me ten minutes to walk there from the road when I went to visit Gemma. It pleased me to think that next time she invited me, I could drive myself. My little car would be dwarfed by the huge old Cotswold mansion, but I'd be proud of it all the same.

So why would GB Bus and Coach have a list of random rural bus stops for a region that their buses didn't serve? And why a particular time against each one? 5.30pm, in the case of St Bride's. The receptionist had mentioned their Shop by Bus campaign, but surely that would only run in the region currently served by their buses, not in the territory of rival companies? Then I remembered the alleged dirty tricks campaign against Highwayman by an unnamed party. Could it be GB Bus and Coach, trying to run Highwayman out of business so that they could take over their turf?

So that was it! Gavin Bing could easily distribute branded merchandise to Highwayman passengers to help win their support for the takeover, and no one could stop him. It was perfectly legal to dish out cute bags of sweets in miniature picnic baskets to random strangers. And who wouldn't say yes to one of those? I'd be thrilled to be picked.

Although if I were running the campaign, I wouldn't include fussy net bags of sugared almonds tied up with ribbons. They'd be far too easy to scatter all over the bus floor if the bus jolted over a pothole, as they inevitably did on every journey round our way. No, I'd get some branded packs made up of travel sweets: those round brass tins that they sell in petrol stations.

I checked my dashboard to see whether there was a shelf the right size and shape for a tin of travel sweets, deciding to buy one next time I saw them in a shop.

As I sipped my coffee, I glanced at the final column on the spreadsheet, which showed three or four numbers. Some sort of product code, I guessed – perhaps they were giving different branded items out at different bus stops and tracking them so that later they might tell which gift had gone down best.

If I'd been in charge, I'd have made the codes easier to distinguish. Some were three-figure and some four; they all ended in 10 or 11.

All those digits reminded me to check the time on the digital clock on my dashboard: 08:10. My first thought was to be irritated that the car dealer hadn't bothered to correct the clock, as it was now late afternoon. I had no idea how to reset it. I'd have to look it up in the manual, which I couldn't be bothered to do now. Then I noticed a tiny button which allowed you to toggle the display between date and time of day. I pressed it and immediately the right time flashed up – 15:45. So the clock was correct. The previous display was the date, 08:10, the eighth of October.

Suddenly my hands clenched around the steering wheel. Of course! The numbers in the final column weren't product codes. They were the dates Bing planned to visit those bus stops. I set my coffee cup carefully into the cupholder and seized the stolen paper with both hands. I checked and rechecked the entry for Wendlebury Barrow. The number in the final column was 0210. The second of October. The date Janice Boggins had been poisoned.

30

———

THE RACE IS ON

Why would Gavin Bing administer a slow-acting poison to Janice Boggins? An awful thought dawned on me that I didn't want to believe. He wasn't giving out gift hampers to win passengers' favour. He was using them to murder random passengers of Highwayman's buses so as to damage their reputation. There was nothing I could do to reverse whatever had happened to Janice Boggins. But if my theory was correct, this list suggested Bing had plans to poison more innocent passengers – and if I acted fast, I could stop him striking again.

To my annoyance, the spreadsheet had not been sorted by date, so I had to cast my eye down it to search the next target date.

I soon found the code representing the date that would be forever commemorated on my new driving licence. The location of the bus stop? St Bride's Lane. The bus stop at the entrance to St Bride's School.

As St Bride's was a boarding school, the bus service didn't usually carry pupils or teachers, all of whom lived on site in term-time, but several members of support staff used it every day, such as cleaning ladies and groundsmen. Their safety was just as important as that of the teachers and pupils.

Then I remembered Gemma making me laugh on my last visit to the school with an anecdote about the headmistress challenging the girls to travel as far as they could by public transport as a skill-building exercise. Used to being chauffeured everywhere by their parents or on the school minibus, their sense of direction was atrocious, and they'd driven grumpy geography teacher Mavis Brook nuts with their planning and navigational errors.

If an adult like Janice could be caught off guard when offered beautifully presented sweets in a cute hamper by a strange man, mightn't the girls be equally vulnerable, no matter how many times they'd been told not to do such a thing?

It was time for me to take action to prevent further tragedies on Highwayman buses.

I removed my key from the ignition. I didn't want to lose my licence for using my phone while driving. Then I pressed the speed-dial number for Hector's House. To my relief, Hector answered, rather than Kate or Mrs Wetherley.

'Hector, hi, it's me. I'm in my car.'

Don't tell me you hope I'm not driving, I thought. To my relief, he didn't.

'Hello, sweetheart, everything okay? Did you get that little Panda you fancied? The price seemed very reasonable, and it should be a fun drive. Much more your cup of tea than my big Land Rover.'

'Yes, and it's lovely, thanks, but we can talk about that later. I've just made a horrific discovery.'

The line fell silent, so I continued. 'You know Carol said she saw Janice Boggins talking to someone in a posh car at the bus stop the morning before she died?'

'Ye-es.'

'Well, I know who it is, and what happened. It was the boss of GB Bus and Coach, and he's been going round giving High-wayman passengers his own company's branded merchandise.'

'Yes, but how would that have killed Janice?'

Was he being purposely dense?

'I think he gave her a poisoned picnic hamper to eat on the bus.'

'What, like the Wicked Queen giving Snow White the poisoned apple?'

'Pretty much, yes. Except Bing didn't have to disguise himself as an old hag. And what's more, he's going to do it again, to lots of bus passengers all over the Cotswolds. It's part of his campaign to drive Highwayman out of business, so his firm can take over their routes. Don't you remember someone asking Leif Oakham at the parish council meeting about a dirty tricks campaign against Highwayman?'

'Well, yes, but I got the impression that was mechanical sabotage like puncturing tyres rather than assaults on their passengers.'

'I suspect he was doing that too.'

I could almost hear the cogs in Hector's brain whirring.

'So that's why no one saw her interact with an assailant on the bus,' he said at last. 'Nobody on the bus poisoned her. I still can't believe the bus driver didn't notice she was dead till the end of his shift. Okay, so he might not have heard her cry for help. Why didn't he spot her death throes in his rear-view mirror?'

I shuddered, instinctively glancing in my Panda's rear-view mirror. *Beware of blind spots*, the driving instructor kept telling me. I put my fingers on the corners, making tiny adjustments to frame precisely the view of the rear windscreen. And then I realised...

'Because the driver had a blind spot that concealed where she was sitting. Do you remember me telling you that when I boarded the bus on Monday morning, he stuck his chewing gum on his rear-view mirror? There was already quite a collection there that could have obscured his view of Janice Boggins.'

Hector gasped. 'Oh, my word, Sophie. You've done it again. As soon as you get back, you must call the police and tell them.'

'Yes, I will, of course. But first things first. The thing is, this wasn't a one-off occurrence. I've discovered a string of bus stops where he's planning to do the same again, starting today with the 5.30 p.m. service from the bus stop outside St Bride's School. That's why I'm phoning you now. You can get there a lot quicker than I can. First, can you call the school straight away and tell them under no circumstances to let any of their staff or girls anywhere near the bus stop this afternoon. I'm sure they can get one or two teachers to drive the cleaners and groundsmen home in the school minibus instead. Then call Max and tell him to stake out the bus stop and look out for a big black chauffeur-driven car with the licence plate GB 123, in such a way that he's not visible to its driver from the road.'

Max is the school's security officer.

'Okay, I will do. But without further proof, I can't see we have any concrete grounds to arrest him for anything.'

'You will have if Max witnesses Bing offering you a picnic hamper that contains poisoned food. And if you're the only passenger waiting at the bus stop, he's sure to.'

'You want me to be the stooge?'

'Yes, please. But don't worry, you'll be perfectly safe. He won't know you from Adam and will just take you for a random bus passenger. Accept the hamper he offers you – it'll be important evidence – but just don't eat or drink anything inside it.'

There was a moment's silence as Hector let this sink in.

'Okay, let's do this. God forbid that any of those nice girls or staff should perish. I'll call Max now and then jump in my Land Rover and get over there now. We should be in plenty of time.'

I pictured Hector looking at his watch.

'Oh, and I know Bing won't be there before I am, as when I left GB Bus and Coach's head office, his car was still there, and his chauffeur was on a break.'

'What on earth were you doing at GB Bus and Coach?'

My enigmatic smile reflected in my now perfectly aligned rear-view mirror. 'Just a touch of industrial espionage. I'll fill you in later. Now, over to you. I'll be there as soon as I can.'

'Okay, but drive safely, sweetheart.'

I stuck my tongue out at the phone. I didn't need his driving tips any more, thank you very much. But I said sweetly, 'I'll do my best.'

As I tucked my phone back in my handbag and summoned up the courage to rejoin the motorway, the dark car flashing the blue overtaking one crossed my mind. I wondered how many miles ahead he'd be now. Was there really any truth in the daft old saying, 'Don't break the speed limit, it won't get you there any faster'? Then my smile froze as I realised the dark car had been a black Tesla saloon. I was willing to bet its licence plate was GB 123.

31

RUNNING IN

There didn't seem much point in heading back to Wendlebury when all the action was going to be taking place around the St Bride's Lane bus stop. Besides, an extra witness might be helpful. So, I decided instead to head to St Bride's. I knew a shortcut that would take me a few miles along a single-track country lane with passing places – good practice for my technique in daylight hours and when there'd be little traffic about. Besides, harvesting was long over, and there wasn't much chance of meeting a tractor or other scarily big farm vehicles. I texted my plan to Hector, adding that I'd hide my car just inside the school gates, along with Hector's Land Rover, so it wouldn't just be Max watching over him.

Unfortunately, I took a wrong turning somewhere near Castle Combe and found myself on a long and winding narrow country lane heading due east instead of my intended north-west. (I knew because the sun was low in the sky right behind me.) The wrong road seemed never-ending, and it was completely bereft of places where I might do a three-point turn.

There were hardly any passing places either, making me increasingly nervous.

I was in a cold sweat by the time I reached a crossroads with an old-fashioned wooden signpost sloping at a steep angle to the ground. Feeling dehydrated, I applied the handbrake and upended my coffee cup into my mouth for the remaining few drops.

The left-hand post told me I was eleven and a quarter miles from Tetbury. I glanced at the dashboard clock. It was just gone five, so there was less than half an hour to go before the bus arrived. GB 123 would get there long before me now, without getting lost. Such a fancy car was bound to have a built-in satnav, as well as Mr Memory Man at its helm.

I wiped my forehead with the crumpled tissue on top of my handbag, before realising it was the one I'd used to wipe spilled coffee off the steering wheel earlier. A glance in the rear-view mirror told me I now had brown smears above my eyebrows. This journey really was demonstrating just how useful rear-view mirrors could be.

Flinging the tissue into the footwell of the passenger seat, I wrenched the handbrake off and sped towards Tetbury. The next bend in the road made me gasp and slow down. These roads were not made for fast cars, and this would not be a great time to go careering off the road and land in a field full of sheep. Hector would say it was more important I reached St Bride's in one piece, even though strictly speaking I was surplus to requirements at this stage. Hector, witnessed by Max, would catch Gavin Bing red-handed, and Max, in his inimitable way, would find some way of immobilising him until the police arrived to arrest him. Rumour had it Max was ex-SAS, with enough specialist combat training to overcome any villain. That's why the school employed him, to keep their young charges safe from harm. You couldn't help but feel safe with Max.

What felt like five miles later, I arrived at another white-painted crossroads sign, this time telling me I was ten and three-quarter miles from Tetbury. These were country miles. I had no option but to press on, though I was disappointed to think I would miss all the action.

By twenty to six, I was still a mile and a half from Tetbury, when I encountered the first vehicle I'd seen since I'd joined this lane. Unfortunately, a big black car was heading towards me, so I'd have to reverse. Slowing to a halt, I closed my eyes and braced myself for the challenge. I'd chosen a compact vehicle specifically to make manoeuvring easier, but considering this was my first journey alone since passing my test, a close encounter in a narrow country lane was a major challenge.

As I opened my eyes, I did a double take at the vehicle now bumper-to-bumper with me. I knew that car. Gavin Bing's car. I felt as if I'd just been cornered in a field by a massive, angry bull.

Somehow, Bing must have eluded Max's attempts to detain him and was now on his way back to Casterbridge. I sensed the driver staring at me. Of course! I'd forgotten to factor in the chauffeur. Between Bing and his driver, they could easily have overpowered Max and Hector. I remembered the chauffeur's battered nose and ears, which I'd assumed were from rugby injuries. Now I realised with a start that despite his flirtatious, jokey manner and smart uniform, they might have been acquired through seedy gangland fights. Quite probably, he wasn't just a chauffeur – he was also Bing's bodyguard, wily as Max, and twice his bulk. I had no idea how big or strong Bing was, but with a sidekick like Mr Memory Man, it didn't really matter. And what about poor Hector?

I wasn't going to let this wicked pair get away with overpowering my friends, but I needed to be smart about it. Mr Memory Man could snap me in half with one hand. And Gavin Bing must be not only arrogant, but unhinged if he thought he could get away with wrecking Highwayman's business by poisoning their passengers at random. He'd doubtless show no mercy to me.

The chauffeur started beeping at me, not just the quick, gentle courtesy beep, but long, repeated aggressive blares. I tooted back, my Panda's shrill horn sounding like his horn's baby.

He started jabbing his forefinger at me to reverse, as if I wouldn't have thought of that for myself. With relief, I realised neither of them were likely to know who I was or what I was doing here. Even though the driver had seen my car in the car park, if you drive a Tesla, you're probably not going to take much notice of a little car like mine. Plus, he was wearing shades, and I'd pulled my hair back into a ponytail and slipped on a hoodie when I stopped for coffee, so he might not recognise me as the girl with long loose hair he'd been chatting up at GB Bus and Coach's car park.

Then I remembered the distinctive colour of my car. Once seen, never forgotten. He'd recognise me, all right.

I gave an exaggerated shrug to indicate I was expecting him to give way to me. Besides, there was a passing place not far behind him – closer than the nearest one to me.

The chauffeur's window glided down slowly, presumably electrically powered. After a moment, he stuck his head out.

'Oy! Just reverse, darlin', can't you? Or will I have to come and reverse it for you? If that's what it takes, that's what'll happen.' Then his tone changed to wheedling, and he flashed a phony smile. 'Now, be a good girl, eh? I've got places to go.'

'I am not your darling!' I shouted, although he wouldn't have been able to hear me, as I kept my windows shut. Then I pressed the central locking button to make darn sure he couldn't force me out of the car.

Just then, a gentler toot came from beyond the black car, and I heard a car door open behind it.

'I say,' called a gentle, refined voice.

A flood of relief washed through me as I recognised the voice of Reverend Gerard Murray, vicar of Wendlebury's parish church of St Bride's.

'Is everything all right there? Have you broken down? Can I be of any assistance? I have jump leads and a tow rope in my boot for just such emergencies.'

The chauffeur's door opened, and I saw him climb out and swagger to the car behind.

Taking my chance, I jumped out of my car and leaped onto the ledge at the bottom of the Panda's door to give myself some height. I waved one arm to get the vicar's attention while holding tight with the other. I didn't want to lose my balance or my dignity by tumbling off into the hedgerow.

'Vicar, it's me, Sophie Sayers!' I shouted. 'Get back in your car, lock the doors and don't move. I'll explain later. Just trust me.'

When the vicar's car door slammed shut, I jumped down and climbed back into the Panda, pressing the central locking button as soon as my door was closed. Then Gavin Bing stepped out of the back of the Tesla.

'You told my driver your name was Martha Boggins? Why, you lying little—'

Beeep! I sounded my horn to drown out his insult.

I scrabbled in my handbag for my phone, keeping it beneath the steering wheel in the hope that he wouldn't see what I was doing, and crossing my fingers that we weren't in a black spot for mobile phone signals.

'Wow, that was quick!' I said a moment later, as blue lights flashed in my rear-view mirror and blaring sirens broke the rural peace. I hadn't even finished dialling 999.

A patrol car pulled up behind my Panda, and two officers, a man and a woman, got out and strolled and bent to look at me through the driver's door window. The woman, who seemed to be the senior officer, motioned to me to open my window, which I did.

'Good evening, madam,' she said, her voice strong and authoritative even in those three words.

'Would you like to see my driving licence?' I said in a small high-pitched voice, wondering whether they'd believe me when I said it was in the post. I'd been given a temporary licence by the test centre to tide me over.

'No need, thank you, madam. Please don't be alarmed. You've done nothing wrong. It's these two gentlemen in the car in front of you that we've come to apprehend, following a tip-off after an incident nearby. But I see you've kindly apprehended them for us. How thoughtful, madam.'

I beamed. 'Yes, I suppose I have. With a little help from my friend, the Reverend Murray, behind him.'

Having heard the sirens, the vicar had been emboldened to leave his car and skirt around the Tesla to join us.

'Good evening, officers!' The vicar gave a friendly wave. 'As I always say, Sophie, "God moves in mysterious ways, His wonders to perform." Don't you agree?'

'You'll be giving the young lady ideas above her station,' said the senior officer with a wry smile. 'Now, gentlemen, let's be having you.'

She stepped past my Panda and approached the black car, in which the chauffeur and Gavin Bing were now slumped in the front seats, arms folded in a sulk.

'I am arresting you in association with the murder of Janice Boggins...'

32

BANGED UP

'And then the police car turned round in the passing place, and I did the most perfect three-point turn.' I was perching on the tearoom counter, swinging my legs as I addressed my captive audience of Kate, the vicar, Mrs Wetherley, Max, Carol, Ted and, of course, Hector.

'She did, you know, she's very good,' put in the vicar.

I took another swig of my comforting hot chocolate. 'Thank you, Vicar.' I gave him my most grateful smile. 'But I couldn't have captured them without you blocking their escape at the rear.'

The vicar waggled his head modestly. 'Ah well, God gave me the strength. I never do anything alone.'

Hector lowered the ice pack from his forehead. 'I could have done with you and God at the bus stop, Vicar. I would have come off a lot worse if Max hadn't leaped out of the bushes just as that gorilla took a swing at me. My own stupid fault for having given the game away by shrinking back instinctively when Mr GB held out the picnic hamper. He must have known from the look of horror on my face that I knew his true intention. I'm sorry, Sophie.'

I jumped down from the counter to give him a consoling hug, avoiding the lump on his right cheek and the bruises where he'd fallen backwards onto an angular edge of the concrete bus shelter.

'Never mind, at least we've put an end now to his appalling shenanigans,' I assured him. 'Goodness knows how many more people he might have killed if you and Max hadn't ambushed him.'

Max gave a hollow laugh. 'Hardly an ambush, Sophie. Now, if you want to hear about a real ambush...'

All the eyes in the room turned upon him. Rumours abounded about the school security officer's past, but he kept his résumé under wraps. And he wasn't about to change. He glanced at the wall clock.

'Must get back to school. Girls won't guard themselves. Duty calls.'

He'd only come back to the shop at Kate's insistence to tell us the full story of what happened at the St Bride's Lane bus stop.

Seeing the pair of them staggering about at the roadside after the attack, the driver of a passing car had called an ambulance, which had escorted them to Slate Green Cottage Hospital. After they'd both been given the all-clear, Kate had collected them in her car. The passer-by had also called the police, describing the attack and the vehicle he'd seen speeding away in a cloud of burned rubber. A patrol car had been sent immediately to chase it, catching up with it in the lane where I was blocking its path a couple of miles away.

'I'll run you back to school, Max,' Kate offered, returning her empty tea things to the counter. 'Ted, can you please come with me and drive Hector's Land Rover back? It's still tucked away behind Max's lodge house. And Hector, darling, I'll be back in the morning to open up with Mrs Wetherley, so you and Sophie can restore yourselves with a nice lie-in.'

'Oh, don't worry about me, Kate.' I beamed, jumping down from the counter. 'I'm absolutely fine.'

'Adrenaline' was the last thing I remember Max saying before I fell to the floor in a faint.

33

FULL CIRCLE

As ever, Kate got her way, and next morning Hector and I were able to sleep in, knowing Hector's House was in safe hands. Everyone had agreed I shouldn't spend the night alone in case I passed out again, and that Hector should be monitored around the clock for signs of concussion. We didn't object. If we both keeled over at the same time, Blossom would have to revive us.

I brought in extra pillows from the bed in the spare room so that we could prop ourselves up comfortably while drinking mugs of comforting tea. Blossom snuggled between us, purring contentedly at having companions for her mid-morning snooze.

'So, did anything interesting happen while I was away?' I asked Hector, craving a bit of normality after all the excitement. We'd had no time since I'd got back from Dorset to catch up on Hector's news or the latest village gossip. 'I'm half-hoping you'll say no. A little boredom would be rather restful.'

Hector tickled me in the ribs, and Blossom gave him a half-hearted swipe with her front right paw for disturbing her peaceful slumber, but she kept her claws to herself.

'I hope you're not calling me boring. Or perhaps I shouldn't worry if it's boredom you're craving.'

I stroked the soft fur at the back of Blossom's neck, comforting us both. She resumed her purring.

Hector caught and held Blossom's tail, which was thumping the duvet every now and again, as if to make sure we couldn't ignore her.

'Sorry to disappoint you, but there was a bit of excitement yesterday morning when Carol's ring turned up.'

I rolled my eyes. 'Don't tell me – she'd put it on the R shelf and forgot about it.' Carol displays her stock in alphabetical order.

Hector laughed. 'I wish it had been that simple, for the sake of all concerned. No, the police returned it to her in a clear plastic bag.'

'Don't tell me Norman had stolen it after all? How disappointing, especially after Kate told us he'd been released without charge. Although he wasn't on the run at all but had just gone to stay with his sister in Dorset to apply for a driving job with GB Bus and Coach. I saw his name in their visitors' book, which he'd signed a few days ago.'

Sighing, Blossom stretched out her front paws, then arched her back. She knew how to take up a lot of space in a bed.

Hector reached for his tea and took a sip. 'You'll be glad to know he didn't steal Carol's ring. It turned up while you were away, and you'll never guess where they found it. I'll give you a clue: it wasn't in Carol's shop. Well, it probably was for a moment, then out in the road, then at the bus stop, then in Slate Green, then back again, then off again...'

I snuggled further under the duvet, watching raindrops pattering on the bedroom window. 'What? You mean it hopped on the bus and bought a ticket? Maybe you are concussed after all. That was a nasty blow to your head last night.' I held up my hand in front of his face. 'How many fingers can you see?'

He covered my hand with his and lowered it onto the duvet. 'I'm perfectly fine, and believe it or not, your guess is nearly right. During the special post-mortem, they discovered the ring in Janice Boggins' stomach.'

'What?' My shriek startled poor Blossom. She jumped up in protest, leaped off the bed and went to curl up on the window seat, nestling against my handbag, which I'd dumped there the night before. 'You mean Janice ate Carol's ring? Why on earth would anyone do that?'

I'd heard of circus sideshow acts eating nuts and bolts but never valuable jewellery.

With Blossom out of the way, Hector wriggled over to close the gap between us and put his arm around my shoulders.

'Current thinking is she palmed it while Carol was picking up Norman's change from the floor. She must have put it in her mouth to conceal it, then accidentally swallowed it.'

I shuddered. 'That must have hurt. Wouldn't it have been easier to hide it in a pocket?'

'The police thought of that. But her coat didn't have any pockets.'

'Ugh, I hate clothes without pockets,' I said. 'I'm surprised it didn't sever her insides and make her quietly bleed to death. Her fellow passengers might not have noticed internal bleeding. It's not as obvious as, say, a stab wound. Or maybe it did damage her insides, but the poison finished her off first. Goodness, fancy dying of two different causes at the same time.'

Hector pulled his arm away in mock horror, and my head fell back against the bank of pillows. 'Sophie Sayers, you ghoul!

No, apparently that had nothing to do with her death. It seems it's possible to swallow a diamond ring and have it pass through the system unscathed. You just need to be patient and it will turn up again, eventually, if you get my drift.'

I wrinkled my nose. 'At least it only got part way through Janice's system. I expect the police gave it a thorough clean before they returned it.'

Hector picked up my left hand and gazed at my empty ring finger. 'Well, she's wearing it again, so whatever they did was enough to satisfy her.'

'What did the police make of it? They could hardly press charges now.'

Hector took a sip of tea. 'Their main concern was to divest themselves of responsibility for the ring. Turns out it was the real thing after all, worth over ten thousand pounds.'

I nearly spilled my tea down my nightie. 'Wherever did Ted get that sort of money? Is he a secret, eccentric billionaire?'

'No, he just struck it lucky with the Premium Bonds, in which he has a modest investment. Whereas most people receiving that kind of win might splash out on a new car or a fabulous holiday, Ted only wanted to find Carol the best engagement ring his money could buy. Oh, and there was enough left over to pay for their wedding and honeymoon. They've set the date towards Christmas, by the way.'

'Wow, how lovely for them both. So, the cause of Janice's death is still poison, then?'

'Yes, but they're not sure how Bing administered it. There was such a cocktail of ingredients in her stomach that they couldn't quite decide the vehicle of the poison. She'd eaten an apple. That's how Alan Turing killed himself, you know – he laced an apple with cyanide, according to urban myth, at least.

It's meant to give off a telltale aroma of almonds. In theory, that would go well with apple – as Mrs Wetherley and Ted would tell you, it's a classic combination in baking.'

I sat up and thumped my right fist on the duvet, unfortunately landing on Hector's stomach. He groaned, but I was too excited to sympathise.

'Almonds!' I declared. 'It was in the sugared almonds, of course. Between the nut and the first layer of sugar. Oh, Hector, don't you see? Cyanide smells of bitter almonds. The receptionist at GB Bus and Coach was adding net bags of sugared almonds to their gift hampers when I visited. No one can eat a sugared almond quickly, can they? You just keep sucking them until the sugar dissolves. They could be anywhere on the journey when the poison took hold, and because it's cyanide, death would be almost instant. And if he only poisoned one or two almonds in every bag, it might be hours or even days before the intended victim succumbs. Or they might not even open the bag on the bus but save them for later.'

'In which case, they wouldn't die on the bus but elsewhere, and Bing's bizarre plan to wreck Highwayman's reputation by murdering its passengers wouldn't work. Old Bing didn't really think his wicked scheme through, did he?'

'I guess he just expected everyone would tuck into them straight away. Maybe he's a greedy creature himself and assumed his passengers would behave the same way he would.'

'That makes perfect sense, Sophie. But how on earth could you prove it?'

'Because I've got one of the net bags of almonds myself.'

'What, he tried to poison you too? When? Where?'

'No, Bing doesn't even know I have it.' I pumped the air in triumph. 'Because his dopey receptionist gave me one in sympathy, when I was putting on my grief-stricken niece act. I'm pretty sure she didn't know what was in them. She seemed genuinely kind. She'll probably be mortified when she finds out what he's had her doing. Hasn't he made her an accessory to murder? That'll cure her crush on him.'

'Poor woman,' said Hector. 'I hope he'll have the decency not to take her down with him. Technically I suppose she *is* an accessory to murder if she's been packing the hampers with toxic treats.'

Then he sat up sharply and took my face in his hands, his eyes wide with terror. 'Sophie, you haven't eaten any of them, have you?'

Putting my hands on his, I gently lowered them into my lap. 'No, of course not. How stupid do you think I am? No, they're safely tucked away in my handbag until I can give them to the police as evidence.'

'Your handbag?' His voice rose an octave between the two words.

I laughed. 'No, Lady Bracknell's line is "A handbag", not "Your handbag". I should know; I was prompt for a month for Damian's production of *The Importance of Being Earnest*.'

Hector opened his mouth to speak, but nothing came out. Then the penny dropped, and we leaped out of bed at the same moment. I ran to the window seat and seized Blossom in my arms, clutching her to my chest and murmuring words of reassurance. Hector grabbed the handbag by the strap and hurled it into the empty open fireplace, before dragging the bedside table to block off the hearth, as if expecting the bag to come to life and try to escape.

'And there it can stay until the drugs squad, or whoever the police send to deal with hazardous materials, can remove it safely. Now, get dressed, we're going back to mine. And close the bedroom door so that Blossom can't possibly get so much as a whiff of the sugared almonds.'

I smiled. It was the first time he'd ever shown any genuine affection for Blossom. If he did ever move into my cottage, I thought all three of us would be okay.

34

THE HIGHWAYMAN DELIVERS

A fortnight later, we were all back in the village hall for another parish council meeting. Only this time it wasn't billed as an emergency meeting, but an extraordinary one, held to bring the community together to share exciting news.

Leif Oakham was speaking to a rapt audience.

'Following the arrest of Gavin Bing, I'm relieved to reveal what I knew about his dirty tricks campaign to scupper Highwayman's bus service in the Cotswolds. I had suspected and now have evidence that the unprecedented series of mechanical failures on our buses lately were due to malicious tampering. The culprits were members of our staff who had sadly allowed themselves to be corrupted by Bing's huge bribes. That was just one way he hoped to close our business down, leaving the routes ripe for GB Bus and Coach to take back, after we'd won it away from them.

'The second prong was his charm offensive, chatting up solitary passengers at bus stops and giving them generous gifts, such as branded shopping bags and purses filled with gift vouchers.

'When these tactics seemed to be working well for him, his arrogance made him take a step too far – way too far. He began a third campaign to murder passengers at random, thinking the association of suspicious deaths on board Highwayman buses would deter passengers from travelling with us, causing us to withdraw our services, leaving room for GB Bus and Coach to expand their empire into the Cotswolds. His weapon: gift hampers, containing poisoned sweets. But this is where his insane scheme backfired. Although he had already given out several of these hampers prior to his attack on Mrs Boggins, she was the only one to die on a Highwayman bus.'

Leif Oakham went on to remind us that headline warnings on every national and local newspaper and on broadcast and social media had ensured all of Mr GB's gifts had now been traced and removed by police specialists. The crisis had been averted. Sugared almond manufacturers had been responding with bitter complaints that one man's reckless behaviour had possibly ruined their businesses for good.

'Unfortunately, Mrs Boggins wasn't the only victim,' he continued. 'Other recipients died elsewhere, either because they didn't eat their sugared almonds until after disembarking or they regifted them to a friend or family member, with tragic results. One lady crushed them with a mallet on her bird table, with the inevitable suffering for her feathered friends. Another set his aside for his mother's birthday present.'

'Cheapskate,' murmured Billy.

'At least his parsimony saved his life,' observed Kate.

'But nothing could save poor Mrs Boggins,' said the vicar, raising his hand. 'My dears, I am at a loss to understand how any business rivalry could justify such a callous, reckless campaign. Why, if each recipient had been as greedy – I mean, as grateful, as poor Janice, Mr Bing would now be classed as a serial killer. What an appalling waste of human life.'

Leif Oakham swallowed.

'I'm afraid Mr Bing was a desperate man. He had confided in me at an industry conference a couple of years ago, before Highwayman ousted him from the Cotswolds, that he had been diagnosed with a terminal illness, details of which I'm sure will soon emerge in the press. I suspect he wanted to secure the future of his rapidly shrinking company for his surviving heirs, whatever it took. He knew that if his crimes were detected, by the time it came to trial, he would be unlikely to live long enough himself to serve any prison sentence. But I will say no more of that for now, out of respect for the professional that he once was, building his own company, as I am building mine, many years ago. Doubtless it will come out in his obituary.'

The room fell silent while we all processed this new development.

Norma Cuts was the first to snap out of it, calling from the front row, 'So where does this leave our bus service?'

Leif Oakham bestowed a smile that showed he'd forgiven her militant campaign. 'I'm pleased to say my board has decided to reprieve the number 27 for the foreseeable future.'

He raised a hand to quell the roar of approval. 'The route still won't be profitable, unless more of you use it, but we have many busy urban routes in our portfolio that pay us big dividends, so it seems reasonable and decent for us to subsidise the 27, and other less populous rural routes. What's more, we have vacancies for a new driver for it since we had to part company with its latest one for gross misconduct.'

'So, the 27 won't be running till you find one?' said Billy. 'Huh! I don't call that a happy ending.'

A man's hand went up in the second row, a hand that was being forced up by a well-manicured lady's hand.

Kate got to her feet, hauling Norman Arch up with her. 'Mr Oakham, I don't think you have to look very far for an experienced driver, do you? Not even beyond the village hall?'

'I could start tomorrow, sir,' said Norman Arch. 'I'd love to work for Highwayman again.'

Leif Oakham looked from Kate to Norman and back again, as members of his audience began to bellow their support.

'Norman Arch! Norman Arch! Norman Arch!'

Leif Oakham gazed about the village hall, absorbing the strength of feeling. Then he smiled. 'I think that's settled. Norman, please call my HR department tomorrow to sign a new contract for an immediate start. And if you're as good a driver as everyone here seems to think, I'd like to talk to you afterwards about getting involved in my pilot programme for autonomous buses.'

Carol, sitting next to me, nudged me in the ribs.

'See, I told you, Sophie,' she hissed.

I raised my hand, and Leif Oakham signalled to me to speak.

'Mr Oakham, could you please explain to me just what you mean by an autonomous bus?'

He nodded, beaming, clearly pleased to be asked to expound on his pet project.

'Why, of course. It's a driverless bus that makes its own decisions, optimising fuel consumption and safety. There are already autonomous buses operating in other parts of the country, for example across the Forth Bridge in Scotland. My ambition is to bring autonomous bus services to more complex, challenging routes such as winding rural Cotswold lanes.'

Hector, on my other side, put his hand up. 'So, does that

mean Norman's new job may be short-lived? Will this autonomous bus ultimately make him redundant?'

Leif Oakham was now in his stride about his favourite topic. 'That's a popular misconception, sir. An autonomous bus requires not only an operative in the driver's seat, but also a bus manager to interact with passengers. So, in the scheme of things, it's a job creation scheme.'

Saxon Arch, sitting next to Norman, waved his arm.

'I'd be interested in that job, if you're offering,' he ventured. Perhaps he'd finally accepted that his driving instructor business was not the success he had made it out to be.

'My HR department can tell you more,' replied Leif Oakham. 'Feel free to call them at any time. But finally, I have one more announcement before the meeting closes. When I said earlier that my board would like to subsidise the 27 for the foreseeable future, I didn't mention why, out of all the troubled rural bus services, we'd chosen Wendlebury Barrow's. But I can tell you now, it's because of one person's appeal in particular.'

Norma Cuts, sitting at the end of the front row, got to her feet and held her placard aloft, beaming. Leif Oakham ignored her.

'It was a moving letter I received from a remarkable young man in your community,' he continued.

Norma's placard clattered to the floor as she sank back into her seat.

'It was from a young man in the throes of his first romantic relationship with a young lady resident of Slate Green. He said without the 27 bus, his heart would break, as he'd be isolated forever from the one he loved. His charming missive reminded me of how I felt, growing up in an isolated village not unlike Wendlebury Barrow.'

'Tommy! You old softie!' cried Billy, slapping his thighs in his mirth.

A groan came from the back of the hall, where Tommy was perched on the top of the Wendlebury Players' lighting ladder. He couldn't have been more conspicuous as a sea of faces turned to gaze up at him in astonishment. There was literally nowhere for him to hide up there, so he had to make do with covering his blushes with his hands.

The audience went wild.

'Well done, lad!'

'Go, Tommy!'

'You're a hero, son!'

Gradually Tommy slid his hands away from his face, uncurled his back and sat up straight and proud, his arms aloft to acknowledge the applause.

'That's my brother, that is!' shouted Sina, pointing, as if there was anyone in the village who didn't already know. Everybody laughed and cheered for her too.

Later, as we left The Bluebird, where half the village had gathered to celebrate the news, I wondered whether Hector would turn left to come back to mine or head to his flat for the night.

He paused as we reached the pavement and turned to face me, his hands on my shoulders.

'Sophie, while you were away on your driving course, I had a good old chat with Kate, bouncing ideas off her for how to optimise the space in my flat for both living and displaying the second-hand books. She made me realise that if we're going to do it properly, I'll need to give up nearly all my living space. Although outside of opening hours I'll still be able to use the fireside chairs and the sofa and so forth, it won't feel the same. It'll be like sleeping in the shop. So, Kate suggested... I was wondering if it mightn't make more sense... I mean, it really hit home when Norman was going on about how lucky we were to have a house each. I mean, if you were up for it, of course...'

I'd let him flounder enough.

'Would you like to move in with me?' I tried to sound innocent, hoping he hadn't guessed I'd planted that idea with Kate. 'Would that solve the problem?'

His shoulders sagged with relief. 'Well, if you're offering...'

I threw my arms around his neck, and he hugged me tight.

'Okay, partner!' I cried.

We were both laughing as Kate came towards us from the pub door, wheeling her electric bike down the path that led to the High Street.

She winked at me. 'Everything okay, Sophie?'

I grinned. 'Yes, it is now. Thanks, Kate.'

She gave her most gracious smile, mounted her bicycle and sailed off into the night, spokes purring like a kitten in the evening breeze.

ACKNOWLEDGEMENTS

In a curious example of life imitating art, not long after I started plotting this story, the bus company serving my home village in the Cotswolds announced it was cancelling our local bus route, although without the kind of mayhem that Sophie Sayers and friends experienced with Wendlebury Barrow's number 27. If this book helps persuade real-life bus companies of the importance of rural routes and encourages them to retain essential services to isolated rural communities, I shall be very glad.

My experience as a bus passenger and as a driver in the narrow country lanes that criss-cross the Cotswolds gave me plenty of material for this story. I'd also like to thank local driving instructor Rob Phillips for his advice about intensive driving courses, and for his perfect put-down line: 'That's why they call them crash courses.'

It's been so long since I learned to drive that by now, my instructors will have died of old age. If not, and, Mick Frost, you're reading this, thank you for equipping me to pass my test second time round in your smart little Datsun Cherry.

I'm not so thankful to my previous instructor, Gary, who regularly proposed to me on my lessons. After several weeks of stonewalling him – as I kept my eyes on the road, of course – he phoned to tell me his car had broken down beyond repair, so he was giving up teaching. I didn't believe him.

I'm grateful to the kind examiner who apologised for failing me first time around and told me I'd be a better driver as a result. He was right. The examiner on my second test was similar to Sophie's, shouting at me not to dither. Assuming I'd already failed, I put my foot down and tried to get through the rest of the test as quickly as possible. To my great relief, I passed.

On a more practical note, huge thanks to my daughter Laura for typing up my manuscript. I write my first drafts by hand in fountain pen – if you'd like to know why, there's a post on my blog about it here: https://authordebbieyoung.com/2019/09/18/handwriting-books-fountain-pen/. She also provided some invaluable feedback and suggestions to improve the story, before it went to my editor at Boldwood Books.

Finally, as ever, I am enormously grateful to the whole team at Boldwood Books for turning yet another of my mad story ideas into a beautiful book to share with the world.

Rachel Faulkner-Willcocks has been a brilliant and supportive editor and mentor. Copy editor Becca Mansell has worked wonders untangling the knots in my timeline and spotting continuity errors, and proofreader Debra Newhouse has played detective tracking down any remaining issues and adding the final polish.

Ongoing and undying thanks to Boldwood's marketing team, led by Nia Beynon and Jenna Houston, for sharing this book with the wider world.

I'm enjoying every minute of this journey.

Debbie Young

ABOUT THE AUTHOR

Debbie Young is the much-loved author of the Sophie Sayers and St Bride's cozy crime mysteries. She lives in a Cotswold village, where she runs the local literary festival, and has worked at Westonbirt School, both of which provide inspiration for her writing.

Sign up to Debbie Young's mailing list for news, competitions and updates on future books.

Visit Debbie's Website: www.authordebbieyoung.com

Follow Debbie on social media:

X x.com/DebbieYoungBN

f facebook.com/AuthorDebbieYoung

BB bookbub.com/authors/debbie-young

⊙ instagram.com/debbieyoungauthor

ALSO BY DEBBIE YOUNG

A Gemma Lamb Cozy Mystery

Dastardly Deeds at St Bride's

Sinister Stranger at St Bride's

Wicked Whispers at St Bride's

Artful Antics at St Bride's

A Sophie Sayers Cozy Mystery

Murder at the Vicarage

Best Murder in Show

Murder in the Manger

Murder at the Well

Springtime for Murder

Murder at the Mill

Murder Lost and Found

Murder in the Highlands

Driven to Murder

Poison & Pens

POISON & PENS IS THE HOME OF
COZY MYSTERIES SO POUR YOURSELF
A CUP OF TEA & GET SLEUTHING!

DISCOVER PAGE-TURNING NOVELS FROM
YOUR FAVOURITE AUTHORS &
MEET NEW FRIENDS

JOIN OUR
FACEBOOK GROUP

BIT.LYPOISONANDPENSFB

SIGN UP TO OUR
NEWSLETTER

BIT.LY/POISONANDPENSNEWS

Boldwood

Boldwood Books is an award-winning fiction publishing company seeking out the best stories from around the world.

Find out more at www.boldwoodbooks.com

Join our reader community for brilliant books, competitions and offers!

Follow us

@BoldwoodBooks

@TheBoldBookClub

Sign up to our weekly deals newsletter

https://bit.ly/BoldwoodBNewsletter